BBC CHILDREN'S BOOKS

UK | USA | Canada | Ireland | Australia
India | New Zealand | South Africa

BBC Children's Books are published by Puffin Books,
part of the Penguin Random House group of companies
whose addresses can be found at global.penguinrandomhouse.com

www.penguin.co.uk
www.puffin.co.uk
www.ladybird.co.uk

First published by Puffin Books 2011
This edition first published by Puffin Books 2016

001

Written by Steve Lyons
Copyright © BBC Worldwide Limited, 2016

Printed in Great Britain by Clays Ltd, St Ives plc

A CIP catalogue record for this book is available from the British Library

ISBN: 978-1-405-92259-3

All correspondence to:
BBC Children's Books
Penguin Random House Children's
80 Strand, London WC2R 0RL

BBC

DOCTOR WHO
TERMINAL OF
DESPAIR

Steve Lyons

PUFFIN

Contents

Contents

Chapter 1
Arrivals

'I think we've landed in an airport,' said Amy.

The Doctor peered out of the TARDIS from behind her. 'Oh,' he said. 'Sorry about that. Come back inside. I'll try again. Better luck next time.'

'Er, not so fast, if you don't mind,' said Amy. 'We're here now. What's wrong with having a quick look around?'

They were in a long, large well-lit hall that was lined with luggage carousels. Most of the carousels were stationary, but the one at the far end was turning. A lone black sports bag sat on it, going round and round in endless circles.

The Doctor frowned. 'You want to see more of this? Why?'

'Because it might be interesting, that's why,' said Amy. 'What do you have against airports?'

'Not only airports,' said the Doctor. 'It's bus stops, train stations, ferry terminals. Anywhere people gather and just . . . wait.'

'Right,' said Amy. 'I get it.'

'They're hardly places at all really, are they?' said the Doctor. 'They're just the places between other places – other, more interesting places. Isn't that right, Rory?'

Amy's husband had appeared in the TARDIS doorway. He looked nervous. Rory wasn't as comfortable travelling in space and time as the other two were.

'You know, Doctor,' said Amy, 'people do use public transport. We can't all go whizzing about the universe in a super-duper police box.'

'Why is there no one around?' asked Rory.

The Doctor gave a disinterested shrug. 'Maybe it's night-time and there are no flights till morning. Maybe they've closed this terminal.'

'You said we'd landed in an airport, right?' said Rory. 'I heard you say that.'

Rory had noticed something the Doctor and Amy hadn't. Almost hidden behind the TARDIS was a small, round window. It looked out upon a vista of stars.

Amy saw it now too, and she grinned with excitement.

'I don't think we're in an airport,' said Rory.

'Space,' said Amy. 'We're in space. So this must be a *space*port!'

'I can hear voices,' said the Doctor, and he shot off across the baggage claim hall. Amy and Rory trailed after him.

'I hear them too!' Amy said, as they passed through an open and unstaffed security gate. They found themselves in a huge, open area full of red plastic seats. There were scores of people – ordinary human beings – milling about.

'This'll be the departure lounge, then,' said Rory.

The lounge was dominated by a curved outer wall studded with airlock doors and portholes, through which they could see outer space. Great spaceships floated behind three of the portholes. They were attached to the airlocks by thick white tubes.

'There,' said the Doctor, 'do you see now? All these people, and not one of them wants to be here. They all want to be somewhere else.'

'They do look pretty miserable,' said Rory.

'I don't blame them,' said Amy. She pointed to a monitor that hung from the ceiling. 'Look at the departures board. Every flight out of here is delayed.'

'Delayed, you say?' asked the Doctor. 'How interesting. No, really – I think that's incredibly interesting. I'm so glad we came here and saw that. Now, can we leave?'

He turned and marched back the way they had come. When he saw that his friends weren't following him, however, he stopped and turned back round.

Amy had spotted a bright yellow shop sign at the far end of the lounge. It read: TERMINAL 4000 DUTY-FREE STORE.

'We have got to look in there,' she said. Then, noticing the Doctor's sulky expression, she pleaded, 'Ten minutes. No, five, tops. Come on, Doctor, we're in the future. I just want to see what a duty-free shop looks like in the future.'

The Doctor sighed and nodded. 'Five minutes,' he said.

'You heard the man, hubby dearest. Let's go!' Amy took Rory's hand and dragged him after her as she ran to the shop.

The Doctor was bored. He paced up and down. He clicked his tongue impatiently.

He wondered how long his friends had been gone. He checked his watch. It had been almost a minute.

Someone had left an old paperback book on one of the plastic seats. It was a whodunit. The Doctor liked whodunits.

4

He sat down, picked up the book and began to read. He skimmed the first three pages. He stopped and frowned. He flicked to the last page of the book, glanced at it and sighed. 'I knew it,' he said to himself.

A woman was standing nearby, watching him.

'Hello,' said the Doctor.

She looked surprised that he had noticed her. 'Hello,' she said, approaching the Doctor shyly.

She was young, with short, dark hair. She wore a red and purple uniform. 'I'm the Doctor,' said the Doctor. 'And you must be . . . ?'

'Janie Collins,' said the woman. 'I'm a flight attendant with Orion Spaceways. I haven't seen you here before.'

'No. That's probably because I haven't been here before. I'm just passing through, really. You aren't going to make a fuss about passports or tickets?'

'Were you sent by the spaceport company?' asked Janie.

'I'm not sure,' said the Doctor. 'I don't think so.'

Janie's face fell. 'Then you haven't come to save us?'

'Oh, well now, that's a different question altogether,' said the Doctor. He dropped the book and bounced to his feet. He took Janie's hands and fixed her with his most reassuring stare. 'You see,' he said, 'saving people just happens to be what I do. Can't help

5

myself. So, tell me, Janie – what do you need saving from?'

The duty-free shop had been trashed.

Amy and Rory stood in the doorway, staring at the mess. Shelving units had been knocked over. The tills had been wrenched open and emptied.

'Who could have done this?' asked Amy.

Rory shrugged. 'Maybe we should find a security guard.'

But Amy wanted to explore for herself. She took a few steps further inside the shop. Her foot crunched on something. She had stepped on a broken perfume bottle.

'Amy, wait,' said Rory. 'Do you hear that?'

Amy stood still and listened.

From the back of the shop came a snuffling sound. Some expensive handbags were piled up on the floor, and Amy realised that the pile was moving.

She felt a chill run down her spine.

'There's something in here with us,' she whispered.

'You're different from the other people here, Janie,' said the Doctor.

'Am I?' said Janie.

'Oh, yes,' said the Doctor. 'Look at them. Look at

their faces. They're all so gloomy. They need a good . . . I don't know, a good singalong or something.'

'I don't think that would help,' said Janie.

'Well, maybe not. But you – you chose to come over here. You spoke to me. These others – if you look, Janie, if you look very carefully out of the corners of your eyes, you can see them. They don't want us to know, but they're watching us.'

'They're as curious as I am,' said Janie. 'They're wondering if you can save them too, but they don't dare ask.'

'Why not?'

'They're afraid.'

'Afraid of what?'

'Afraid to hope.'

'Yes, I think I see,' said the Doctor. 'No. Wait. No, I don't see, in fact.'

The young flight attendant sighed. 'We've all been here so long. I was supposed to be working the 2345 flight to Calisto.'

'Was that at eleven last night?' asked the Doctor.

Janie looked at him strangely. 'Last year,' she said. 'There's only one flight a year to Calisto, and mine was due out in October of 2345. That was five months ago.'

The Doctor looked at Janie. He blinked.

'I'm sorry,' he said. 'I must have misheard you. I thought you said five months.'

'I did,' said Janie.

'But you meant five months as in . . . ?'

'As in five months,' said Janie.

'Let me get this straight,' said the Doctor. 'You've been waiting here, in this spaceport terminal, for a hundred and fifty-one days *in a row*?'

'We've nowhere else to go,' said Janie. 'Terminal Four Thousand is an interchange station. There's no access from here to any world. The only way out is by ship – and no ships have left since the monsters appeared.'

The Doctor's expression brightened. 'I owe my friends an apology,' he said. 'There is something to see here after all. Tell me all about these monsters, Janie Collins!'

Amy could see it now. It was a squat, grey creature, the size and rough shape of a small, fat dog. It was lying in the debris of the duty-free shop. It didn't seem to have noticed her.

'Be careful, Amy,' whispered Rory.

Amy took a step towards the creature. Its nose and ears twitched, and it stood up. It had a stumpy tail and three stubby legs, one at the front and two at the back.

'It's all right,' said Amy. 'It's a dog. Well, a sort of a dog. It looks a bit like a bulldog – y'know, that same little scrunched-up face?'

Rory craned to see from behind her. 'Yeah, I think I saw . . . there were two or three others like it out in the departure lounge.'

'There you are, then,' said Amy. 'I bet three-legged alien dogs are this year's must-have pet. This one must be lost, the poor thing.'

'Doesn't mean it won't bite,' said Rory.

But Amy wasn't listening to him. She crouched beside the dog and tickled its chin. 'Hello, boy,' she said. 'What's your name, then?'

The dog looked at Amy for a moment.

Then it roared.

A green and slimy tentacle shot out of the dog's mouth. At the tip of the tentacle, there was a second, smaller mouth. This mouth had two tiny rings of sharp teeth, and it was slavering and hissing.

The dog-monster leapt at Amy. She shrieked. Its claws pinned her shoulders to the wall, and the mouth on the tentacle darted towards her throat.

Chapter 2
Who Let the Dogs Out?

Amy could feel the dog-monster's hot breath on her face.

She fought as hard as she could, her arms flailing about, and caught the creature's chin with her right elbow. Its head snapped to one side. It whimpered. The slimy tentacle mouth had just missed Amy's throat, but she was still pinned to the wall. She tried to push her attacker away from her, but it was too strong. Its claws were digging into her flesh.

'Rory!' she yelled. 'Do something!'

The Doctor heard an animal roar from inside the duty-free shop. An instant later, he heard a shriek.

'Amy!' The Doctor began to run towards the duty-free shop. Janie grabbed his arm and pulled him back. 'No, Doctor, you can't!'

He brushed her hand away. 'Can't do what?' he snapped. 'Can't go to a friend in need? You'll find I very much can.'

'You can't help her,' said Janie. 'You mustn't even hope you can, or they'll get you too!' She was clinging to the Doctor again.

'Now, that –' he began. He had meant to say something angry, but midway through the sentence he stopped. He frowned in thought. 'That doesn't make any sense at all, actually. Unless . . .'

The Doctor was missing something.

He closed his eyes and concentrated. He replayed the last few seconds in his mind. He looked for details he hadn't noticed the first time.

His eyes snapped open. 'The dogs!' he exclaimed.

He whirled round. There were two grey three-legged dogs behind him. The Doctor had seen them before, but hadn't paid them much attention. They had just been mooching about the departure lounge.

They were certainly interested in him, though.

As soon as the Doctor had started towards the duty-free shop, the two dogs had perked up. They had begun to approach him, cautiously; they were wary of him. They had stopped a short distance away and were watching the Doctor closely.

He turned to Janie and whispered, 'It's them, isn't it? The dogs. They're your monsters.'

Rory didn't know what to do.

He never knew what to do in situations like this. His every instinct was telling him to run, but he couldn't leave Amy.

He grabbed the first thing to hand – a small, round bottle of perfume – and ran at the dog-monster, screaming.

The scream was actually a sort of war cry, meant to give Rory confidence. He also hoped it would distract the dog from its victim. It did.

The dog let go of Amy. It dropped back on to all three of its feet. Rory had intended to get right up behind it and hit it with the bottle, but, as the dog turned his way, he lost his nerve. He threw the bottle instead.

He missed the dog.

The perfume bottle smashed against the wall. Its green liquid contents exploded across the shop, making everything smell of some alien flower.

The dog growled at Rory.

He backed away, holding his hands up. 'There, there,' he said. 'Nice doggie. Good doggie. Sit, Fido, sit. No – stay, Fido, *stay*!'

The dog had tensed as if to spring at Rory.

But, instead, it convulsed in what looked like a sneezing fit. Some of the spilled perfume must have got up its nose.

Rory took the opportunity to dash to Amy's side. He grabbed her hand, and they ducked behind one of the few shelving units still standing, then crept round the edge of the shop, giving the sneezing dog a wide berth. At last, they saw a clear path back to the door.

Amy had been splashed with the perfume too. She wrinkled her nose at the smell. 'Mmm,' she said. 'My new favourite scent. How did you know?'

'Call it husbands' intuition,' said Rory.

'You spoil me.'

'We *are* still technically on our honeymoon,' said Rory, as they hurried out of the shop.

The passengers in the departure lounge were afraid.

They were edging away from the Doctor, clearing a space around him. Only Janie remained at his side.

The Doctor took out his sonic screwdriver and aimed it at the two dogs in front of him. Janie gasped with delight. 'You have a weapon!'

'I wouldn't call it a weapon exactly,' he confessed. 'More a *tool*. A really useful tool, but all the same . . . Okay, a screwdriver. It's a screwdriver.'

Janie's face fell.

'But it's a *sonic* screwdriver,' said the Doctor, 'and that makes it cool, I think.'

The two dogs were circling him, in opposite directions.

Janie shouted at the onlookers, 'Help him, somebody. Can't you help him?'

'The thing about dogs is,' said the Doctor, 'they have brilliant ears. Much better than human ears. They can hear all sorts of things we can't. Of course, these are alien dogs, so their ears might be different. But if I can find a sound frequency they don't like . . .'

The dogs started growling. They edged closer.

The Doctor quickly shut off the sonic screwdriver.

'Ah. Right,' he said. 'Attracting them instead. Best not to do that, then.'

Janie tried again with the passengers. 'The Doctor's here to help us,' she cried. 'He says he can get us out of here, but he won't be able to if we let the Desponds have him. Don't you think it's time we stood up to them? Don't you think it's time we –'

The two dogs sprang at the Doctor and Janie.

Amy raced out into the departure lounge, leaving Rory struggling to close an automatic sliding door behind them that was out of power and didn't want to be closed. Amy cried out for the Doctor, then halted in her tracks.

The Doctor was being attacked, too. He had grabbed a red plastic chair and was using it to fend off another of the alien dog-monsters.

Beside the Doctor, another dog had knocked a young flight attendant to the ground. She was screaming, but no one made a move to help her.

Rory reappeared at Amy's side.

'Perfume,' said Amy. 'We need more perfume!'

Rory groaned as Amy pushed him back towards the duty-free shop.

The door was jammed not quite shut. There was a small gap that was too tight for Amy to get through – and that meant it was too small for the squat dog-monsters, too.

Rory peered through the glass, looking for the dog he had trapped inside the shop. 'I don't see it,' he said.

The dog sprang out from behind an overturned shelf. It threw itself at the door and smacked into the glass. Rory started and backed away quickly.

The creature had hurt itself. It staggered away, back into the shop, dazed.

Amy strained at the door. 'If we can budge this a couple of centimetres,' she said, 'I can wriggle through and grab –'

She realised that Rory wasn't listening to her – he was looking at the Doctor.

They were too late.

The Doctor's attacker had suddenly backed off.

He jabbed the red chair in the dog-monster's direction as a warning. 'Ha!' he shouted.

He had always fancied himself as a lion tamer. *Why have I never been a lion tamer?* he wondered. Too cruel to the lion, he supposed.

The dog lay down on its stomach. That was not what the Doctor had expected – the dog had gone from trying to bite him to ignoring him.

Janie hadn't fared as well. She was on the floor, the other dog standing on her chest. A tentacle had shot out of its mouth and attached itself to Janie's throat.

The Doctor prodded the dog with his chair. 'Shoo,' he said. 'Go on, shoo!'

He succeeded in dislodging the creature.

He'd expected it would be angry with him, but it just slunk away.

The Doctor crouched beside Janie. She was still awake, but dazed.

'Hmm, you don't appear to be injured,' he said. 'There's a big red suction mark on your throat, but the skin isn't broken. Weird. You've had a lucky escape, I'd say.'

He helped Janie to her feet, as Amy and Rory ran up to them. Rory warily skirted the dog that had attacked the Doctor. It had fallen asleep.

'What did you do to that thing?' asked Amy. 'Why did it back off?'

'Wish I knew,' said the Doctor.

'Does it matter?' asked Janie, with a shrug. She began to walk away.

The Doctor stopped her. 'Whoa,' he said. 'Where do you think you're going?'

'I need a lie-down,' said Janie.

'I thought you were going to help us. You were going to tell me about these dog things.'

Janie brushed the Doctor's hand off her shoulder. 'What's the point? What can you do? What can anyone do? You should have been here five months ago, Doctor. We needed you then. It's too late now. They've grown too strong.'

The Doctor stared into Janie's eyes. 'You weren't lucky at all, were you? That monster did something to you. No, wait, I'm wrong. It *took* something from you.'

'Of course it did,' snapped Janie. 'Why do you think we call them –'

'Wait a second,' said the Doctor. 'Oh, oh, oh, I think I'm getting something! Something somebody said.' He slapped himself on the forehead. 'Lion tamers! Did someone mention lion tamers? No? That must have just been me, then.'

The Doctor clicked his fingers. 'I've got it. Desponds! That's what you called them, before they attacked us: Desponds!' The grin faded from his face. 'Which is what you were just about to say, isn't it?'

'Desponds?' repeated Amy. 'As in despondent?'

'Dejected. Down in the mouth. Lacking in hope. And you, Janie Collins, you were so full of hope a few seconds ago, but now . . . That's what they took from you, isn't it?'

'Doctor, what are you saying?' asked Rory.

'I'm saying these Desponds feed off human emotions, and one emotion in particular,' replied the Doctor. 'They've been preying on the people in this spaceport terminal. They've been sucking the hope right out of them!'

Chapter 3

Nature of the Beasts

Janie shuddered at the Doctor's words.

Obviously he had guessed right.

An older couple came forward. The woman wrapped a red tartan blanket round Janie's shoulders and murmured comforting words to her.

'Just one more question,' said the Doctor, as the couple led Janie away. They ignored him, so he turned to address the departure lounge in general.

'One question,' he said. 'Just one. How many of these Desponds are there?'

'Twelve.' The answer came from behind the Doctor.

He turned to see a black-uniformed man leaning

against a wall. He was young and lean, with tightly curled hair and a thin moustache.

'Twelve,' the Doctor repeated. 'Thanks. And you would be . . . ?'

'Roger. Roger McDowell. I'm with Spaceport Security.'

'Security. Yes. I guessed you might be, what with, you know, the uniform and the yellow badge on your arm that says SECURITY. I'm observant that way.'

'There were thirteen Desponds,' said Roger, 'but I shot one, once.'

'Well,' said the Doctor. 'Good. That's good for you, Roger.' He punched the air in an attempt at a gesture of solidarity. 'Well done.'

The Doctor had always been uncomfortable around guns.

Amy was looking at Janie Collins. The older couple had guided her to one of the red plastic chairs and were fussing over her. They had found her a plastic cup of hot water.

'That could have been me,' said Amy.

Rory reassured her. 'But it wasn't.'

'It gives me goosebumps thinking about it,' said Amy. 'Imagine what it must feel like to have a part of you just . . . sucked away.'

The Doctor leaned in between them. 'That's enough moping around,' he said. 'Monsters to deal with. Twelve of them.'

'That's, er, eleven now,' said Rory. 'I trapped one in the duty-free shop.'

The Doctor was already marching away. 'Back door!' he called over his shoulder.

'Oh,' said Rory.

Amy ran after the Doctor. 'What's the plan?'

'Don't know yet,' said the Doctor. 'But it's bound to be good.' He took out the sonic screwdriver and clicked it a few times. 'I expect there'll be sonicking involved.'

The Doctor spied a drinks machine. It was empty. He had Rory help him to turn the machine round, then he used the sonic screwdriver to unscrew a back panel.

Amy spotted another Despond padding towards the three of them. 'Doctor . . .' she said.

The Doctor had yanked a handful of circuit boards out of the drinks machine. He bundled them into Rory's hands and continued to work as he talked.

'Ah. Okay,' said the Doctor. 'I suggest no one makes any sudden moves, and . . . and try to worry.'

'You mean try *not* to worry,' said Amy.

'Oh, crikey, no. That would just be reckless!'

'Ah,' said Amy. 'Right. I see . . . I think. The Desponds feed off hope. They're attracted to it. So, we have to, er, *not hope* and they should leave us alone.'

'Take your cue from your other half here,' said the Doctor. 'He's a natural born worrier. Right now, he's convinced we're all going to die. Isn't that right, Rory?'

'No,' said Rory defensively. 'That's not what I was thinking. I was just –' he started, and then realised what he was saying. He looked at the Despond. 'I mean, yes, Doctor,' he said woodenly. 'We're all going to die. Not the slightest doubt about it.'

'Never mind,' said the Doctor. 'You can work on it. For now, I think the Desponds are more curious than hungry. They've just fed on Janie's hope, after all.'

'One of them did,' said Amy. 'Only one of the Desponds attacked Janie. That still leaves the other eleven.'

'But remember the dog that attacked me,' said the Doctor. 'Remember what it did.'

'When the other Despond fed on Janie, yours just gave up,' said Amy.

'As if it was full up too,' said Rory.

'A psycho-empathic link between the pack!' announced the Doctor. Amy had no idea what that meant, but the Doctor explained. 'When one of them feeds, they all feed.'

'And when one of them gets hungry . . .' said Rory.

The approaching Despond roared.

Out came the slimy tentacle with the second mouth on it.

'Okay,' said Amy nervously. 'Didn't take too long for dinner to go down . . .'

The Doctor leapt up, brushing his two friends aside. He was holding a wire in each hand. The wires trailed back to the drinks machine.

The Despond came galloping at the Doctor and launched itself at his throat.

The Doctor ducked beneath the monster's feeding tentacle and thrust the two wires into its stomach. There was a bright flash, a sizzle and a horrible smell of burnt fur.

The Despond hit the floor with a thud.

It wasn't seriously hurt, though; it scrambled to its three feet and backed off, whimpering.

Amy noticed that a couple more Desponds not far away were also looking groggy. 'I think that electric shock affected all of them,' she said.

'Thought it might,' said the Doctor, 'if only on an emotional level. Should keep them at bay for a while, anyhow.'

At that moment Janie reappeared, and made her

way over to the Doctor and his friends. Her shoulders were still stooped, her eyes downcast.

'I wanted to apologise,' Janie said. 'I was rude to you back there.'

'Hardly your fault,' said Amy, who was surprised to see the flight attendant again. 'You'd had a pretty nasty shock.'

'If anyone should be sorry,' said Rory, 'it's the Doctor.'

'Er, standing right here,' said the Doctor.

'I just mean,' said Rory, 'you're the one who gave her hope, and that's what attracted the Desponds to her. That's how it works, right?'

Janie pulled up a chair and sat down. 'It was nice, though,' she said, 'to dream about getting out of here, just for a while. I'd forgotten what it was like to dream.'

The older couple who had been helping Janie had followed her over. Now the woman placed a hand on Janie's shoulder. 'There, there, dear,' she said. She had silver hair and broad shoulders. She wore a floral-patterned orange dress, and clutched a matching handbag to her breast. 'Things aren't so terrible here, are they?'

Her partner was heavy-set, balding, with a grey moustache and steel-rimmed glasses. 'Mrs Henry is right,' he said. 'We have a roof over our heads, and heat and light and water. There are far worse places than this.'

Amy couldn't believe her ears. 'All the same,' she said, 'you must want to go home.'

'What about food?' asked the Doctor. 'You must be running out of food.'

'It's true,' said Mrs Henry. 'We have emptied the food court.'

'And the shops,' the old man added. 'And the dispensing machines.'

'But we've heard a rumour, Mr Henry and I,' said Mrs Henry.

Mr Henry checked over his shoulder for eavesdroppers. 'We have heard there might still be coffee and biscuits in the first-class passenger lounge.'

'And frozen fruit!'

Mr Henry shushed his wife fiercely.

'I'm sorry, dear,' she said, shamefaced. 'I was hoping for too much.'

'You see,' said Janie, 'the Desponds have fed on all of us, and some of us many times.'

'They've made us afraid to hope,' said Mrs Henry.

'And what's the point of hoping, anyway?' asked Mr Henry.

'One of the guards – young Roger – shot a

Despond once,' Mrs Henry recalled. 'But he used up all his bullets.'

'We hoped the spaceport company might send someone,' said Janie.

'But we're so far away from any world here,' said Mr Henry.

The Doctor straightened up and clapped his hands. 'Right,' he said. 'Heard enough. More than enough. A piece of advice, Janie Collins, Mr and Mrs Henry: you might want to steer clear of me, because right now I am the most dangerous person in this room. Ask me why!'

No one asked the Doctor why.

The awkward silence lasted for at least five seconds before Amy rolled her eyes. 'Why?' she asked.

'Because Rory was right,' said the Doctor. 'The people I call my friends, the ones who really get to know me, there's one thing they can't ever do and that's give up hope. Impossible situations? I get out of four every day before breakfast. Unbeatable odds? I beat them in my spare time. Invincible –'

'We get the point,' said Amy.

'As for last-second saves,' said the Doctor, 'they're my speciality.'

'So what do we do?' asked Rory.

'We get everyone out of here,' said the Doctor.

'We can't,' said Janie. 'Terminal Four Thousand has been placed under quarantine.'

'No ships come here any more,' said Mr Henry. 'They haven't for –'

'Five months,' interrupted the Doctor. 'I know. One thing. One teeny-tiny little thing – well, three things, really.' He marched along the departure lounge. He pointed to the three portholes in turn. Or, rather, *through* them to the spaceships beyond.

'Don't you think that, if escaping was so easy, we'd have done it long ago?' asked Janie.

'Those ships are the ones that brought us all here,' said Mrs Henry.

'They're held by the spaceport's docking clamps,' said Janie. 'They can't be let go until they're cleared for departure. And they can't be cleared until –'

'Until the quarantine is lifted,' guessed Rory.

'Well, then,' said the Doctor. 'Sounds like a plan to me. Lifting the quarantine – who do we see about that?' He answered his own question. 'No one here from the spaceport company, so the systems must be automated. From where, though? From Space Traffic Control, of course. And that would be . . . ?'

There was another awkward silence.

'No, really, I'm asking,' said the Doctor. 'I don't know.'

'I could show you to the control tower,' said Janie. 'I suppose.'

'Good,' said the Doctor. 'Right away, then, please – before the Desponds decide to feed again.'

'We can keep them away now though, with those wires,' said Amy.

The Doctor shook his head. 'As the Desponds grow hungrier, they'll become more determined. And the three of us – you, Rory and me – we're the only people here they haven't already fed on.'

'We're fresh meat!' Rory realised.

'We'll be like beacons to the Desponds,' said the Doctor. 'We'll be great big, juicy, hope-filled, packed-with-crunchy-goodness beacons!'

Chapter 4
Taking Control

The Henrys decided to stay in the departure lounge. 'It's what we're used to,' said Mrs Henry. 'Our own two rows of chairs, with our coats and towels to sleep under, and the washrooms across the way.'

'And, frankly, after all you said,' said Mr Henry, 'about the danger . . .'

'We'd just . . . Mr Henry and I, we'd rather not get our hopes up.'

'I'll leave Rory with you,' said the Doctor, 'in case.'

'In case of what?' protested Rory. The Doctor was already hurrying away after Janie. 'In case of what?!' Rory shouted after him.

Amy had hung back. She looked at Rory sympathetically.

'Go on,' said Rory with a sigh. 'Go after them. It's

fine. I'll just stay here. With the Henrys. And the monsters. *In case.*'

Amy caught up with Janie at the security gate. The Doctor had rushed ahead, but didn't know which way to go; he had to stop and wait for Janie to catch up and show him.

Janie glanced at the TARDIS as they passed it, but didn't ask about it. She led the way back through the baggage claim hall, round a corner and into a wide concourse.

There were two Desponds here. They had knocked over a queuing system in front of a row of check-in desks and were playing with the ropes and pillars.

When they noticed the newcomers, however, they stopped playing and turned to watch them.

To take her mind off the creatures, Amy turned to Janie. 'You know,' she said, 'you surprise me. In a good way, I mean. To be helping us out like this, after what the Desponds . . . that must be wearing off now, right? You must be feeling a little bit hopeful again, or else why –'

'There is no hope,' said Janie.

Amy eyed the two Desponds. 'No,' she said, pulling a gloomy face. 'No, of course not. No hope.'

'I'm only taking you to Space Traffic Control,' said

Janie, 'so you can see that for yourself. Don't make the
same mistake we made. You don't want to fight back.
The sooner you accept how things must be, the easier
it will be for you.'

There was a door in the far wall. Its latch was
broken. Janie led the Doctor and Amy through it and
up a spiral staircase that opened out into a circular
room with portholes all round it, looking out into
space.

'Here it is,' said Janie. 'The control tower. Do you
see what I mean now?'

Amy looked around Space Traffic Control in
dismay. She saw exactly what Janie had meant.

Rory sat on a red plastic chair, glaring at a Despond.
It was mooching around, a little too close to his feet for
comfort.

Something of a buzz had gone up around the
departure lounge. A knot of people had formed by the
bureau de change and they were talking in low voices.

Mr Henry had gone over to see what they were
saying. 'There's a raid planned,' he whispered when he
returned, 'on the first-class lounge.'

Mrs Henry clapped her hands together. 'Oh, how
wonderful!'

'A raid?' said Rory. 'But why? What for?'

Mr Henry glared at him. 'For the coffee, of course. And the biscuits.'

'It really is unfair,' said Mrs Henry. 'We're so hungry out here – there's hardly any food left – but in there . . . Who is in there these days, Mr Henry? I forget.'

'It must be Captain Stone's group,' said Mr Henry. 'I haven't seen them around in a while. Yes, I'm sure that's right. They won the last raid, remember?'

'I can't believe I'm hearing this,' said Rory. 'Listen to yourselves. Haven't you got enough to worry about without fighting each other?'

Mr Henry shot Rory a warning glare, and Rory looked over his shoulder. The Despond he had been watching was ambling towards him.

'He'll understand, dear,' said Mrs Henry to her husband. 'Once he's been here as long as we have. Once the Desponds have fed on him two or three times.'

The Despond was still approaching, now with more purpose.

Rory leapt to his feet. He addressed the Despond as firmly as he could. 'No,' he said, 'you don't want to feed on me. I . . . I'd probably give you indigestion.'

Mr Henry shook his head. 'The classic mistake,' he said.

'I know, dear,' his wife sighed. 'Hoping they won't attack him.'

'And, of course, that hope attracts them all the more.'

'I'm a pessimist,' insisted Rory. 'Ask my wife. Ask Amy. If it wasn't for her . . . she's the only reason I'm travelling with the Doctor. Last-second saves? Really? He's let me die more than once. Long story. I'm just saying.'

He was backing away slowly, towards the gutted drinks machine with its trailing wires. He was hoping to . . .

No, Rory told himself sternly. *Don't hope!*

Too late. Another Despond had appeared behind him and was cutting him off from the drinks machine.

Rory picked up a chair. It was no use, though; he knew he couldn't fend off two of the creatures at once.

'I imagine this is why the Doctor left you with us, dear,' said Mrs Henry.

'Yes,' said Mr Henry. 'He knew you could lead the Desponds away from us.'

The creatures were almost upon Rory now. He threw the chair at the nearest of them and ran for it. The two Desponds went barrelling after him.

'What happened here?' cried the Doctor.

'Well, obviously,' said Janie, 'other people had the same idea as you.'

The Doctor massaged his temples as if he had a

35

headache. 'No, not the same,' he moaned. 'Not the same idea at all. I wasn't planning on wanton vandalism!'

There were instrument banks all the way round the room. They had been wrenched open, and the wires pulled out of them. Monitor screens had been smashed, indicator lights shattered. It reminded Amy of the damage to the duty-free shop.

'We came here months ago,' said Janie. 'We tried to get the computers to release the docking clamps on the passenger ships.'

'By smashing everything to pieces?' said Amy. 'Good plan!'

'We couldn't find the security codes,' said Janie. 'People got frustrated.'

The Doctor had already slid under one of the consoles. He was using the sonic screwdriver to repair some broken wires.

'Didn't you hear me?' said Janie. 'Even if you could fix the controls –'

'The Doctor can fix them,' interrupted Amy.

'Even if he does,' Janie went on, 'we don't have the codes to access the computers.'

'One problem at a time,' came the Doctor's muffled voice from beneath the console. 'Amy, keep an eye on the stairs. Let me know if any Desponds –'

He broke off in mid-sentence, as there was a sudden *pop* and an electric flash.

'Doctor!' cried Amy. 'Are you okay? What happened?'

She heard a rumbling sound behind her and whirled round. A security door had just slammed down over the exit.

The Doctor sat up and blew ruefully on his fingers. 'I think I may just have reactivated a system I shouldn't have reactivated.'

Janie sank into a chair. 'I knew something like this would happen,' she said despairingly.

'Doctor,' said Amy, 'can you hear that sound? A sort of hissing?'

The Doctor's face lengthened. 'Ah.'

'Ah what?' said Amy. 'What does "ah" mean? "Ah" doesn't sound good.'

'I think . . .' said the Doctor. 'Now, Amy, don't panic, but I think I may have just triggered a security lockdown. And, in fact, I think –'

Janie doubled over, coughing. Amy's throat was itching, and her eyes were beginning to water.

'You see,' said the Doctor, 'the main computer has detected an unclassified alien life form in this room, which would be me, and so it's –'

'It's disinfecting the control tower!' gasped Amy.

She barely got the words out before she too had a coughing fit. She could hardly breathe.

Amy could see a metal grille in the wall, near the floor. The hissing was coming from down there. *It's pumping gas into the room*, she realised. *Invisible poisonous gas!*

And she, the Doctor and Janie were trapped in there with it.

The Doctor stood up and aimed his sonic screwdriver at the security door. It whined and glowed a fierce shade of green, but nothing else happened. The door stayed closed. The Doctor groaned.

'Deadlock sealed!' he said.

Amy had an idea. She shrugged off her baggy jumper, and dropped down by the grille in the wall. She stuffed her jumper into the grille to block it up.

'Nice thinking,' said the Doctor. 'Should slow down the inflow of gas, at least. Otherwise try breathing through a hanky, if you have one. Oh, and stand on a chair.'

'What?'

'The gas is heavier than air,' said the Doctor. 'It's filling the room from the bottom.'

'Right,' said Amy.

She didn't have a handkerchief, but Janie had two moist towelettes. Amy took one gratefully, and pressed it over her nose and mouth. She climbed up on to a chair and pulled Janie up after her. It didn't seem to help much.

Amy felt as if tiny claws were tearing at her throat. There were hot tears streaming down her cheeks. 'What about you, Doctor?' she croaked.

The Doctor shrugged. 'Doesn't seem to affect me,' he said. 'There's no reason why it should, of course. A Time Lord's physiology is very different to –'

'Great,' said Amy. 'I mean, that's really great for you, considering the whole point of this is to – what was it again? Oh, yes – kill the alien life form!'

The Doctor grinned. 'Ironic, isn't it?' Then he became serious. 'Of course, that's how we fix this!' he said. 'That's how we get the lockdown lifted.'

'How?' asked Amy.

'Obvious, isn't it?' said the Doctor. 'We give the computer what it wants.'

'But doesn't it want –'

'The computer wants me dead,' said the Doctor. 'So, to get you and Janie out of this room, it looks like I'll have to die.'

Chapter 5
The Doctor Dies

Rory pelted across the departure lounge with one of the pursuing Desponds snapping at his heels. *It's going to catch me*, he thought. *I know it is! Where's the Doctor when I need him?*

The creature fastened its teeth round Rory's trouser cuff. It tugged, and he lost his balance and fell over.

Rory's hands and knees slipped on the floor tiles, as the Despond dragged him backwards. He went on the offensive: he bopped the Despond on its scrunched-up nose. It recoiled, and Rory scrambled to his feet.

The other Despond was charging at him, its feeding tentacle extended.

He ducked behind a young woman in a fur coat. She shrieked as she saw the two Desponds coming at her. 'I'm sorry,' said Rory, mortified. 'I didn't mean –'

Of course, the woman was in no danger. It was Rory the Desponds wanted; anyone else was just in their way.

He gained a little ground on them as they dodged round the shrieking woman. He knew it wouldn't last, though. The Desponds were faster than he was.

Rory heard a voice calling, 'Over here!'

It was Roger, the security guard he had met before. He was standing in the doorway of the men's washroom, beckoning to Rory urgently.

Rory had no better ideas; he ran into the washroom, the Desponds right behind him. Rory slammed the door in their faces and fell back against it breathlessly. He could hear the Desponds scratching on the other side of the door, and one of them howled.

Rory turned to Roger, to thank him for his help.

He froze as he saw that Roger was holding a gun on him.

'Doctor, what . . . what are you saying? What . . . ?'

Amy couldn't speak any more. She had swallowed too much of the poisonous gas. Her lungs felt as if they were on fire.

'No time to discuss it,' said the Doctor. 'I need you to trust me and to do as I say.'

Amy nodded helplessly.

'In a moment, Amy,' said the Doctor, 'that security door is going to open. As soon as it does, get out of here. Take Janie. Don't worry about me.'

Amy could hardly see. The gas had made her eyes swell up.

She could just make out the shape of the Doctor sitting in a chair. His chin was resting on his chest. He looked like he was going to sleep.

Amy wanted to scream at him, *How can I not worry about you? After what you said, about you having to die* . . . but she was overcome by another coughing fit.

Janie had passed out. She was leaning on Amy's shoulder.

Amy was growing light-headed too. Her legs felt weak. She tried to hold her breath, but she was coughing too much. She couldn't take much more of this.

To her relief, the security door rose.

Amy lifted Janie down from the chair on which they both stood. She dragged her across the room and out through the doorway.

She collapsed on the stairs outside. Fresh air had never tasted so sweet to her. Amy gulped it down by the lungful, feeling stronger with each breath she took.

She remembered the Doctor. He was still inside the control room.

She looked back and saw him. The Doctor was still slumped in his chair. He wasn't moving. Amy couldn't tell from where she was if he was breathing or not.

The Doctor had told her not to worry about him. Easier said than done! Amy had to go back for him . . . but, before she could, the security door slammed down again in front of her nose.

She cried out, 'No!' She hammered on the closed door with her fists. 'Doctor,' she yelled, 'what have you done? Doctor!'

On the other side of the door, the Doctor opened his eyes and grinned. He was very impressed with himself.

His plan had been simple. He had put himself into a trance. A deep trance. So deep that his heartbeats and breathing had been almost undetectable.

He had tricked the main computer into thinking he was dead.

So, of course, it had ended the lockdown. It had opened the security door, and let Amy and Janie go.

Now, the Doctor had come round and the computer had sealed off Space Traffic Control again. It was pumping more poison gas into the room.

That was okay, though, because the gas didn't affect the Doctor. And, although he was still trapped, he was right where he needed to be.

The Doctor flexed his long fingers. It was time to get to work.

'Um,' said Rory. 'Okay. So, obviously, you have a gun.'

'I'm sorry,' said Roger.

'You're sorry. That's good. Well, it's a start. So, why *are* you – I mean, if you don't mind my asking – I don't mean to pressure you or anything, but –'

'We need your help,' said Roger.

Rory was relieved. At least Roger wasn't planning to shoot him. And, anyway, he had just remembered something he had heard earlier.

'I see. Right,' he said. 'And you thought the best way to ask me was at gunpoint?'

He advanced on Roger, holding out his hand. 'Why not give me the gun, and then we can, I don't know . . . talk, I suppose.'

Roger backed away from him. 'Don't come any closer,' he said, 'or I'll shoot.'

'I don't think you will,' said Rory. He was gaining confidence.

'I mean it,' said Roger. 'I shot a Despond once. I killed it.'

'And you used up all your bullets. Mrs Henry told us so.'

Roger turned quite pale. His aim wavered. Rory was right.

Rory smiled as he reached once more for the security guard's gun.

Roger struck like lightning. He turned the gun round and smacked Rory in the temple with the butt end of it. Lights exploded behind Rory's eyes. He felt his legs turn to jelly and saw the tiles on the bathroom floor rushing up to meet him.

It's not fair, he thought as he lost consciousness. He had just been getting the hang of being a hero.

Amy had given up hammering on the security door. She was getting no answer. *Probably soundproof*, she thought – at least, she hoped that was the reason.

Janie came up behind her. She laid a comforting hand on Amy's shoulder. 'Don't worry,' she said. 'I'm sure the Doctor will be fine.'

Amy looked at Janie, surprised. She appeared to be recovering from the Despond's attack; she was beginning to hope again.

Well, if she can do it, thought Amy, *so can I*.

'You're right,' Amy said. 'I've seen the Doctor stand up to Daleks and Weeping Angels. He's alive in there, I know he is, and he's working on a way to help us.'

'So what do we do?' asked Janie.

Amy shrugged. 'I don't know,' she said. 'Find Rory, I suppose.'

The mood in the departure lounge had changed. Amy sensed it as soon as she and Janie walked in. The stranded passengers in the lounge were no longer without purpose. They had formed into groups. They were whispering to each other, plotting. Some of them had armed themselves with chairs or sticks or bottles from the duty-free shop.

'I know this feeling,' said Amy. 'This is like a . . . a rowdy party, when things are about to turn ugly. The Desponds can feel it too. Look.'

They could see five Desponds among the crowd. The dog-like creatures were awake and very much alert.

'They do this,' said Janie, before correcting herself. '*We* do this, every few weeks – more often, since the food has been running out. It's . . . I don't know, I suppose it's a way of releasing the frustration we all feel. They're . . . we're going to war.'

One of the larger groups had just made its move.

At one end of the departure lounge was a marble water feature. In an alcove next to it was an unobtrusive doorway. It had been boarded up with planks from the inside.

'That's the first-class passenger lounge,' said Janie.

Twenty or so people were marching towards the doorway. One of them – a man with a stubbly beard – carried a fire extinguisher, which he rammed into the wooden boards. Amy saw hands reaching through the planks from the other side, trying to push the bearded man away. But the other members of his group were straining forward too, lending their shoulders to the effort.

'Come on,' said Janie. 'Let's get out of here.'

'Wait,' said Amy. 'What about Rory? I don't see Rory. He was with the Henrys. Can you see the Henrys?'

'*Smash it all down!*' A teenager in a combat jacket had leapt up on to a chair. He was punching the air as he yelled, 'Smash down the class barriers. No first class or business class or club class. An end to privilege. Free coffee and biscuits for all!'

A Despond leapt at him. It knocked him off his chair and fed on him – on his hope. It was over before Amy could do anything.

The Despond waddled away, full. The teenager stayed where he had toppled on to the floor. He rolled on to his side and pulled his knees up to his chest miserably.

Apart from Amy and Janie, no one seemed to

notice. The passengers were too busy, surging angrily towards the boarded-up doorway.

Amy was still searching for Rory when she spotted something odd: the security guard, Roger, pushing a luggage trolley across the departure lounge, far from the action. Whatever was on the trolley was covered by a blanket.

Amy heard a terrible splintering sound before she had time to think any more about it. The planks across the doorway had been broken; the way into the first-class lounge was now clear.

The passengers had started to fight with each other in their little groups, each group determined to beat the others through that doorway.

Amy and Janie were caught right in the middle of the chaos.

Chapter 6
Turbulence

Amy kept her head down as sticks were waved and punches thrown around her.

We've got to get out of here, she thought, *before someone gets hurt!* She grabbed hold of Janie's hand and tried to pull her to safety. To her dismay, their path was blocked by a huge, angry-looking woman with some kind of baton – it took Amy a second to recognise it as a metal-detector wand.

Amy squared up to the huge woman, putting on her no-nonsense face. 'Now, look here, um, madam,' Amy snarled. 'We don't want to have to fight you, so why don't you just step of our way and we'll –'

Janie grabbed a luggage trolley and rammed it into the huge woman's shins. The woman whimpered with pain and dropped her weapon.

'Okay,' said Amy. 'That works too.'

They ran past the huge woman, only to find a Despond in front of them, growling.

Janie squealed and ran away from the Despond – right back into the thick of the fighting. Amy was forced to follow her.

The Doctor had lashed a few more wires together. He stood up and flicked some switches on an instrument panel. All around the Space Traffic Control room, monitor screens and indicator lights – those that hadn't been smashed – began to light up.

'Now to get those docking clamps released,' the Doctor said to himself.

His attention was drawn to a bank of twelve screens. Seven were broken, but the other five were showing scenes from around the spaceport: security-camera feeds.

The Doctor saw what looked like a riot in progress in the departure lounge. He ran his fingers through his hair in exasperation. 'What are they doing down there?' he wailed.

He only hoped his friends weren't involved. *They won't be*, the Doctor told himself. *Amy and Rory are too sensible for that.* Then, on a cracked screen, he saw a wave of red hair. Amy. She was right in the centre of things, with Janie. *Of course she is!*

It looked like Amy and Janie were about to get trampled. They needed help – but what could the Doctor do? The security door was still down.

He wasn't able to leave the room.

'Amy, help me!' shrieked Janie. 'I can't get up!'

Janie had fallen over. The heaving crowd closed in around her, and whenever she tried to stand she was knocked down again.

'Take my hand!' Amy urged. She was being pushed and prodded too, but she was determined to stand her ground. She stooped down to help Janie up – and came face-to-face with a Despond.

She froze. She stared at the Despond. The Despond stared back at her. It opened its mouth to extend its feeding tentacle.

Amy forced herself to close her eyes. She thought very hard. *There is no hope,* she told herself – and she tried to make herself believe it. *The Doctor's trapped in Space Traffic Control. I don't know if he's alive or dead. Rory's disappeared and everyone's fighting and the Desponds are everywhere and . . .*

She felt a genuine pang of despair. Perhaps there *was* no hope.

Then Amy heard a cry. She opened her eyes.

The Despond had turned away from her and

clamped its mouth round the leg of a middle-aged man. He was trying to kick the Despond away, but now a second creature bounded to the aid of the first.

The two Desponds dragged the man to the floor. One pinned him down with its claws, while the other went for his throat with its feeding tentacle.

Amy had kept the Desponds from attacking her and, instead, they had found another victim. She felt responsible.

'*Psst!*'

A figure beckoned to Amy from beside the water feature at the end of the departure lounge. It was Mrs Henry. 'Over here, dear,' she called in a loud whisper.

The fighting had shifted away from Amy, as the passengers avoided the feeding Desponds. Janie had managed to get to her feet. She tugged at Amy's arm. 'There's nothing you can do for him,' she said – she must have guessed what Amy was thinking.

'But it's my fault he's –' began Amy.

'No,' said Janie. 'This is what happens. This is what always happens. We think we're safe, because we aren't hoping for much – we aren't hoping for escape or anything like that, just a few little luxuries – but it gets out of hand. We get caught up in the moment. We hope too much . . . and that's when people get hurt.'

The Desponds had finished feeding now. It was too late anyway.

'Better him than us,' said Janie.

She led the way to where Mrs Henry was waiting.

The Doctor sniffed the air. The smell of the poisonous gas had lessened.

'Well, that had to happen,' he said. 'Your tanks have run dry. So, now what?'

He was addressing the computer that ran Space Traffic Control.

'I know you can hear me,' he said. 'You're configured for voice activation. This is your alien infestation here, or "the Doctor" to my friends.'

Letters streamed across a tiny read-out screen:

ALIEN INFESTATION DETECTED. LOCKDOWN IN FORCE.

'Oh, come now,' said the Doctor. 'I know you can do better than that.'

The same message scrolled across the screen again.

'Think about it,' said the Doctor. 'Well, not *think* – I know you can't think exactly – but run this through your processors. You work on logical principles, right? So tell me, what is the logic of keeping me in this room? I'm waiting.'

ALIEN INFESTATION CONTAINED, the read-out said.

'Right. Yes,' said the Doctor. 'I get that. You've contained me. But why?'

AWAITING INSTRUCTIONS.

'No, sorry. Won't wash. There's no one here from the spaceport company. You'll have to follow your existing programming. Your sensors detect an alien life form in this room. So you trap it in here, yes?'

THESIS IS CORRECT.

'Then you kill it. And that's the important part – the killing – because this is Space Traffic Control. It's okay for unclassified life forms to wander about the rest of the terminal, but as soon as one of them gets in here it has to die.'

THESIS IS CORRECT.

'Of course, you don't distinguish between good life forms and bad life forms. No – don't even try to answer that. There's just one little fly in your ointment: me. I'm not that easy to kill. You might have noticed.'

THESIS IS –

'Yes, yes, yes, "thesis is correct". Don't interrupt me when I'm speaking. You see, your programming has failed. You can see that, can't you? You've confined your alien infestation – me – to the last place you want me to be.'

AWAITING INSTRUCTIONS.

'You don't have time to wait,' said the Doctor.

AWAITING INSTRUCTIONS.

'And you don't need new instructions. You just need to apply your logic. You have an alien infestation in here, one you can't seem to kill. For as long as you keep this control room in lockdown, that can't change. But open the security door and maybe – just maybe – the infestation will leave of its own accord.'

The Doctor waited.

The computer didn't answer him.

He sighed. 'I'm sure this used to be much easier. Okay, I'll leave you to ponder that for a moment. In the meantime, I'll see what I can do from in here.'

He walked up to an instrument panel and flicked a switch.

Bang! An electrical charge jolted through the Doctor's body. He was hurled back across the room and into the wall. He slid to the floor and lay there for a second, his eyes closed.

Then his eyes snapped back open. 'So, it's like that, is it?' he said. 'All right, then. This means war!'

'We're so pleased you decided to join us, dears,' said Mrs Henry.

She was standing with her husband and a group of six or seven older passengers. Like the others, they had armed themselves as best they could. Mr Henry had a walking stick, which he waved about vigorously. He almost hit Amy with it.

'Indeed,' said Mr Henry. 'You're precisely what our little group needs: two pairs of younger, fitter hands to fight with us.'

'Now, hang on a minute,' said Amy. 'That's not what we –'

'We're biding our time, you see,' said Mrs Henry.

'We're waiting for the others to tire themselves out,' said Mr Henry.

'And then we'll swoop! It was Mr Henry's idea.'

'That first-class lounge will be ours tonight, you mark my words.'

'We'll have coffee and chocolate biscuits and, oh, flowers and moist towelettes.'

'We're just looking for Rory,' said Amy. 'My husband. He was with you.'

'We haven't seen him, dear,' said Mrs Henry. 'Have we, Mr Henry?'

Mr Henry shook his head. 'Not for some time. Some protector he turned out to be.'

'You must have seen where he went,' said Amy, frustrated.

'I don't think so, dear,' said Mrs Henry. 'Unless . . .'

'Unless?'

A shifty look crept over Mrs Henry's face. 'Unless

Captain Stone took him. Captain Stone and his group. They're in the first-class lounge, you see. They –'

'Uh-huh,' said Amy. 'I think I do see, yeah.'

A group of passengers had forced their way into the first-class lounge. Another group had gone in after them, intent on dragging them back out again.

'And this happens every few weeks, you said?' Amy asked Janie.

'That's right,' said Janie.

Amy nodded. *Makes sense*, she thought. *The first-class lounge is probably in the same state as the duty-free shop – and the Space Traffic Control tower, and most of the rest of the spaceport – by now.*

'So,' said Mrs Henry eagerly to Amy, 'will you help us to take over the first-class lounge or not? You never know, your husband could be in there.'

The problem was, Mrs Henry was right. No one knew where Rory had got to. If he wasn't in the first-class passenger lounge, then where else could he be?

Chapter 7
Engine Failure

Rory opened his eyes. It was dark. His head ached. He was lying on his back on a hard surface under a thick blanket. The blanket irritated Rory's nose. He sneezed.

The blanket was whipped away.

Rory saw the security guard, Roger, standing over him. A memory came rushing back. 'Did you . . . did you just knock me out?' asked Rory blearily. He tried to sit up. To his surprise, Roger knelt to help him.

'It was the only way to get you here,' said Roger.

Rory was on a luggage trolley. It was jammed into an aisle between two columns of fixed seats in a long, narrow compartment. The back of each seat held a folded-up table with a cup-holder.

Roger pulled an oxygen mask down from the ceiling. He handed it to Rory. 'Here,' he said, 'use this. It'll help to bring you round.'

They were on a spaceship, Rory realised. A passenger spaceship.

The fighting had spread all across the departure lounge. The Desponds were having a field day, claiming victim after victim.

Amy was waiting with Janie, the Henrys and their group in the corner by the water feature. Someone had given her a plank to use as a weapon. It looked to Amy like a broken shelf from the duty-free shop.

Most of the passengers had forgotten what they were fighting about. They were lashing out blindly, caught up in the moment, giving vent to their pent-up emotions.

The way into the first-class lounge had been left clear.

Mr Henry raised his walking stick above his head. 'To battle!' he yelled.

His group surged forward, following his lead. Only Janie stayed behind.

Amy was swept along with the others. She didn't want to be there. She didn't want to have to fight. *But what about Rory?* she thought. What if he was in trouble inside that room and needed her?

'Have you asked him yet?'

Rory looked up. A newcomer had just entered the passenger compartment through an airlock at its rear. He was wearing a bulky white spacesuit with a helmet.

'I was about to,' said Roger.

'About to ask me what?' asked Rory. 'Look, where are we, anyway?'

'You're aboard my ship,' said the man in the spacesuit. His voice came out through a speaker in his chest unit.

Rory looked at Roger. 'We aren't . . . ? I mean, we haven't left the spaceport?'

Roger shook his head. 'We can't ship out until the computers release the –'

'The docking clamps. I know.' Rory breathed out, relieved.

'You see, Cap? He knows his stuff.'

The newcomer lifted off his helmet so Rory could see his face. He was probably in his mid-fifties. He was short with leathery skin and deep frown lines around his eyes.

'Cap runs a space charter service,' said Roger. 'At least, he used to run one, until he got stuck here at Terminal Four Thousand with the rest of us.'

'Okay,' said Rory.

'But that's about to change. Cap and me, we've a plan for getting out of here.'

'Good,' said Rory. 'That's great. I'm sorry – can

we fast-forward to the part I still don't understand? That's the part where you beat me unconscious.'

It was the other man – Cap – who answered him. 'Thing is, son,' he drawled, 'I lost my tech guy in a fire-fight with the Sidewinder Syndicate a few months back.'

'So we need a replacement,' added Roger.

Rory stared at the security guard. He wasn't sure if he had heard him right.

Cap was peeling off the rest of his spacesuit. 'I've tuned up my old engines till they sing,' he said. 'A little more juice through the couplings and I figure we'll be there.'

'I still say we could do it,' said Roger, 'with the new fuel mix I suggested.'

'Not worth the risk, son,' said Cap. 'Not now we have the expert here.'

'Expert?' repeated Rory. He blinked. 'You don't mean *me*?'

A new sound rang out through the departure lounge: three melodic chimes, followed by a short burst of speaker static. Then a voice: 'Ladies and gentlemen, your attention please.'

Mr Henry came to a halt. Behind him the rest of his group faltered too. Mr Henry lowered his walking stick and raised his head to listen.

'Orion Spaceways Flight Number Forty-seven departing to Drahva now boarding at Gate Fourteen and a half. This is a final call for Orion Spaceways Flight Number Forty-seven to Drahva.'

Amy could hardly believe her ears. She recognised that voice.

It belonged to the Doctor.

The Doctor was still in the Space Traffic Control room. He was watching the departure lounge on the security-camera screens.

The passengers had stopped fighting. It was as if they had come out of a collective trance. They were looking at each other and up at the ceiling, confused.

Time for another announcement, thought the Doctor.

He operated the tannoy very carefully; he had stripped the insulation from an electric cable and wrapped it round his hand so he wouldn't get another shock.

'All right,' he addressed the departure lounge, 'that was a lie. You probably noticed, there is no Gate Fourteen and a half. And who'd want to go to Drahva, anyway? All those . . . Drahvins. I just wanted to make you all stop and think for a second.'

The passengers were breaking apart. They were picking up their red plastic seats, which had been scattered in the riot. They were sitting down, dispirited.

'Which . . . okay, you appear to have done now,' said the Doctor. 'You've stopped . . . hitting each other with sticks. Well done. So I'll just shut up then.'

The Doctor shut off the tannoy with a scowl. He didn't like what he had just had to do. His plan had worked, though. The Desponds – so excited a moment ago – were slinking away to digest their recent feast. The Doctor had saved the passengers by raising their hopes and then crushing them again.

He switched the tannoy back on. 'I'm so sorry,' he said.

On one of the camera screens, he saw Amy. She looked bedraggled. She had located the camera and was miming something at it. She was asking the Doctor how he was.

'Amy, hold on,' the Doctor broadcast. 'I'm coming down there.'

He stepped away from the controls. He addressed the Space Traffic Control computer. 'Yes, you heard that right,' he said. 'I'm going out there, and I expect you'll probably try to stop me. So. Are you ready for Round Two?'

ALIEN INFESTATION DETECTED, said the read-out screen. LOCKDOWN IN FORCE.

The Doctor smiled grimly. 'That's exactly what I thought you'd say.'

'I keep telling you,' insisted Rory, 'I'm a nurse! I don't know the first thing about –'

'I saw you in the terminal.' Roger had pulled his gun again. 'I saw how you and your friend rewired that drinks machine.'

'Not me and my friend. Just him. Just the Doctor. I was . . . he put some circuit boards in my hands and I . . . look, why don't we go and find him? I'm sure he –'

'Roger,' growled Cap. 'You promised me an engineer!'

'He's lying,' said Roger. He rounded on Rory. 'You're lying! You can't be a nurse! They wouldn't have sent you here if you couldn't –'

'I wasn't sent here!'

'I didn't go to all this trouble for nothing,' snapped Roger. 'You're going to fix up those engines or . . .' He looked down at his gun. His empty gun.

Roger swallowed. 'Look,' he pleaded. 'We're so close to getting out of here. We'll take you with us if you help us. It'll just be the three of us.'

'The three of . . . ?' Rory looked around the empty passenger compartment. 'You could fit about fifty

people in here. Four trips and you'd have the whole of
the spaceport evacuated. Why don't you –'

Cap shook his head firmly. 'That's a bad idea, son.'

'You've seen what they're like in there,' said Roger.
'The passengers. They've been fed on by the Desponds
one too many times. They've no hope left.'

'And you do?' said Rory.

'The Desponds can't get to us in here,' said Roger.

'I haven't stepped outside this ship in two months,'
said Cap proudly.

'I've been out to fetch supplies,' said Roger. 'But
only when the Desponds aren't on the prowl. When
it's safe. That's how we've been able to start hoping
again.'

'We open that airlock door to all-comers and what
do you think'll happen? We'll have them damn dogs in
here faster'n you can say Jack Robinson.'

'We can't take that risk,' said Roger.

'It's a shame about those other guys,' said Cap,
'but, hey, we'll be doing them a mercy. They're all out
of food in there, anyway.'

'What do you mean, "anyway"?' asked Rory.

Roger stared at the floor. He shuffled his feet.
'Well, Cap thinks . . .' he mumbled.

'If we can get that extra juice to the engines,' said
Cap, 'we can tear this ship free of the docking clamps.'

'It's just,' said Roger, 'there's a chance that we'll, um, you know . . . tear a hole in the side of the spaceport too.'

Cap shrugged. 'Like I said, the folks in there, they're all gonna die anyway.'

'You're mad!' cried Rory.

Cap's eyes gleamed fiercely. 'Maybe we are,' he snapped. 'Maybe that's what it does to a man, being stuck in the armpit of the universe for five long months.'

'But you're going to help us,' said Roger quietly, 'or we'll –'

'Or you won't like the consequences!' Cap snarled. He had bundled his spacesuit up into a giant ball, and he now thrust it into Rory's arms.

Rory looked at the spacesuit. He looked at his two captors.

Of course, he thought, with an inwards groan. *The engines must be on the outside of the ship.* He was supposed to put on this suit . . . and walk out into space!

'This day just keeps getting better and better,' Rory muttered.

Chapter 8
The Desponds Feed

'Where are you going?' asked Janie.

Amy halted in her tracks. She turned back to the young flight attendant. 'You heard the Doctor,' she said. 'He's alive. He's on his way down here.'

'So what?'

'So I'm going to meet him. He's probably worked out a way to save us all by now, and . . .' Amy's voice trailed off.

Janie was staring past her, afraid. Amy turned round slowly.

There was a Despond right behind her.

Amy could have kicked herself. The sound of the Doctor's voice had made her hope again. She hadn't been able to help it.

'It's all right,' said Janie, relaxing. 'Look at it.'

'I'm looking,' said Amy. 'Looking right at the monster.'

'It's curious about you,' said Janie, 'but it doesn't want to feed. The Desponds must have overeaten in the riot.'

'So, what, they've all got bellyache?'

'I wouldn't count on it lasting,' said Janie.

'But, while it does, we're safe. We're safe to hope. In which case . . . Janie, come with me. Come and meet the Doctor with me. We can –'

'No,' said Janie. 'I've been fed on once already today. I'll just stay here. With Mr and Mrs Henry and the others. I think that's best.'

'I understand,' said Amy.

'Watch this,' said the Doctor. 'It's going to be good.'

He grabbed an office chair and rolled it on its castors to the edge of the round room. He stepped up on to its seat.

Now he could reach a camera that was hanging from the ceiling.

The Doctor gripped the camera with his hand that was still wrapped in the cable insulation. He wrenched the camera from its bracket and hopped down from the chair.

'Now,' he said, 'unless I've very much missed my

guess . . .' He inspected the device. 'Oh, yes. A body-scanner, X-rays, thermal imaging, the works. Nice. Ideal for detecting, say, unclassified life forms in your control room.'

He looked at the computer read-out screen. It was blank.

'Go on,' said the Doctor. 'Try running a scan now. See what it says.'

Nothing happened for a moment, as if the computer was reluctant to follow the instruction. Then the words appeared: NO ALIEN INFESTATION DETECTED.

'Of course not,' said the Doctor. 'How could there be? I've disconnected your scanner. But that doesn't mean a thing to you, does it? You have your programming. The only thing you care about is –' He pointed to the read-out screen.

NO ALIEN INFESTATION DETECTED.

'And that means . . . ?'

LOCKDOWN LIFTED.

'Good old computer logic!' crowed the Doctor. 'Gotta love it!'

The heavy security door rumbled back up into the ceiling. The Doctor stepped outside and on to the spiral staircase that led back down to the main concourse.

He was four steps down when a thought occurred to him.

'Oh, oh, oh!' cried the Doctor. He whirled round, aiming the sonic screwdriver.

A chair came careering across the control room towards him. At the same time, the computer tried to close the security door again.

The bottom of the door slammed down on to the chair and jammed. There was now a low gap, to each side of the chair, through which a person could crawl.

'Nice try,' said the Doctor. 'You're good, but I'm better.'

Cap's spacesuit was a tight fit on the much taller Rory; he struggled to get his shoulders into it and was disappointed when he succeeded.

Cap lowered the helmet over Rory's head. He fastened the seals on it, then he hefted an air tank on to Rory's back.

Next, Cap attached a flexible tube from the tank to Rory's chest unit. Rory felt a little light-headed as his helmet filled up with oxygen.

He was still terrified about going out into space, even with all this protection. But he didn't know what else he could do, at least for now.

Roger had disappeared into the cockpit of the

spaceship. He returned now – wearing another spacesuit. 'You didn't think I'd let you go out there alone?' His sneering voice sounded inside Rory's helmet, through a radio link.

'Roger here'll be making sure you don't get up to any tricks,' Cap drawled.

'Like what?' asked Rory sullenly.

'Like sabotaging the engines instead of fixing them,' said Roger.

'I wouldn't know how to do either. As I keep trying to tell you –'

'You'll be connected to this ship,' Cap interrupted, 'by a single lifeline. One word over the radio from Roger and –' Cap made a slashing motion with his hand.

'That lifeline gets cut,' said Roger. 'You'll be cast adrift in space.'

'Perfect,' muttered Rory.

Cap led the way to the airlock at the back of the ship. He picked up a toolkit, which he handed to Rory. It was heavier than it looked; its weight almost pulled Rory over.

'You ready for this, son?' asked Cap.

'No,' said Rory.

'Too bad.' Cap wrenched open the airlock door.

Amy met the Doctor in front of the TARDIS. She leapt at him and enveloped him in a tight hug. She knew it would embarrass him, but right now she didn't care.

'Did you do it?' she asked. 'Did you end the quarantine? Can we leave now?'

'Not entirely,' said the Doctor. 'By which I mean . . . well, not at all, actually.'

'Oh,' said Amy.

'Soon, though. Definitely soon. I've been getting the measure of the computer that runs this place. I reckon I can take it!'

The Doctor unlocked the TARDIS door. Amy followed him inside.

They skirted the six-sided console, and headed for an alcove that was cluttered with chests and crates. The Doctor pulled a chest full of junk towards himself. Amy watched as he scattered its contents across the floor.

'What are you looking for?' asked Amy.

'I'll know that when I find it,' said the Doctor.

He finished with the first chest and started on a second.

'Doctor, when you were in Space Traffic Control,' said Amy, 'with the cameras, did you happen to see where Rory might have got to?'

'I hoped you might know,' said the Doctor. 'He's your husband.'

He had found something. It was buried beneath a tangle of wires and circuit boards. The Doctor wrenched it free. 'Oh, yes,' he said. 'This should do the trick.'

Amy craned to see the device. It looked like a metal spider with a keypad on its back. She asked the Doctor what it was.

'An automated safe-cracker,' he said, jumping to his feet.

'Safe-cracker?' echoed Amy. 'For cracking safes? And you just happen to have one of those lying about the place?'

'Why not?' The Doctor grinned. 'You never know when you might have to break into a safe. Or out of one. Did I ever tell you about that time on Fortis Major?'

Amy ignored the question. 'So, what does it do exactly?' she asked instead.

'It runs through about five hundred combinations per second,' said the Doctor. 'Wire this into the computers in Space Traffic Control and –'

'And it'll find the security codes we need to lift the quarantine and release the docking clamps and send everyone home!'

'In forty minutes or less, or your money back.'

'Well, in that case,' said Amy, 'why are we standing here?'

'Of course,' the Doctor added, as they walked away from the TARDIS together, 'we aren't entirely out of the woods yet.'

'What's that supposed to mean?' asked Amy.

The Doctor nodded to their right.

A Despond had just stepped out from between two luggage carousels. Its nose and ears twitched when it saw them.

Amy shook her head. 'It can't be . . . they can't be hungry again already!'

'I suspect,' said the Doctor, 'that the Desponds have a very efficient metabolism. Either that or they found a packet of antacid tablets in the duty-free shop. Amy . . .'

'I remember. Try to worry.'

It worked last time, thought Amy. *Just have to close my eyes and concentrate – tell myself there is no hope. There is no hope!*

'I wasn't going to say that, actually,' said the Doctor. 'What I was going to say is that when I say "run" you should run back to the TARDIS.'

Amy opened her eyes a fraction. 'What do you mean, you *were* going to say?'

'That was before I saw the other one.'

Amy looked properly now. A second Despond had appeared from behind the TARDIS. It was cutting off their way to retreat.

There is no hope, Amy told herself fiercely. But this time it wasn't working; this time, the Doctor was here by her side, so how could things be hopeless?

'Plan B,' said the Doctor. 'When I say "run" you just run. I'll try to draw the Desponds away from you . . . *Run!*'

Amy ran for it. A Despond began to follow her, but the Doctor leapt into its path.

'Here, boy,' said the Doctor. 'Come to me. Not quite so fast —'

Now it was his turn to flee, with both Desponds at his heels.

The Doctor ran for the working luggage carousel and jumped on to it. It carried him away from his pursuers, while leaving his feet free.

The Desponds kept pace with the carousel, snarling and snapping at the Doctor's ankles. He tried to push them away with the soles of his shoes.

One of them leapt up and caught the Doctor's trouser leg between its teeth. It yanked him backwards off his feet. The Doctor landed on his back on the carousel.

The Desponds jumped on top of him. They opened their mouths to reveal their slavering feeding tentacles.

Amy cried out, 'Doctor!' and started towards him.

The Doctor did his best to fight off both Desponds. He pushed the smaller one away from himself; its three paws skittered on the moving carousel and it fell off sideways.

The smaller Despond landed on the floor between Amy and the Doctor. She backed away nervously from it. She had no hope of reaching the Doctor now.

The larger Despond had dug its front claws into its victim's chest. It sank its feeding tentacle into the Doctor's throat. Then both the Doctor and the Despond were carried away by the luggage carousel, through an opening in the wall and out of Amy's sight.

Chapter 9
Once Bitten

Amy eyed the Despond that sat between her and the luggage carousel.

The Despond eyed her in return. Then it stood up and burped loudly, before waddling away towards the departure lounge. It looked a little bit wobbly, as if it had eaten too much.

No, thought Amy. *That can't have happened – not to him!*

She ran up to the moving carousel, as it brought the Doctor round to her again.

He was still lying on his back on the carousel, and he was sucking his thumb. The larger Despond – the one that had latched on to the Doctor's throat – was nowhere to be seen, but in its place was a large red suction mark on the Doctor's neck.

She buried her face in her hands in despair.

The Desponds had fed again. They had taken the Doctor's hope!

Rory was standing inside a tiny airlock. He was elbow-to-elbow with Roger.

Two large coils of cable were fastened to the wall. Roger clipped one cable to a loop on his spacesuit and another to Rory's.

Roger pointed out a tiny explosive charge stuck to Rory's coil of cable. 'One word from me,' he said, 'and Cap will blow that charge from the cockpit. It'll burn right through your lifeline.'

'Yeah,' said Rory. 'I got that.'

For the past two minutes, he had been able to hear machinery: the grinding and wheezing of an air pump. Now the pump shut off with a final clunk.

It had done its job. A gauge on the wall showed that there was no atmosphere left inside the airlock. Rory and Roger's oxygen tanks were the only things keeping them alive. Rory swallowed nervously.

The spaceship's artificial gravity had also been shut off, and Rory was floating. His heavy toolkit was floating too, no longer weighing him down.

Roger spun the locking wheel of the outer airlock door, then pushed the door open. He took the hesitant

Rory by the arm . . . and gave him a decisive push, out
into space.

'Doctor, please,' Amy pleaded. 'Get up!'

She managed to drag him off the moving carousel,
but it was like handling a rag doll. He sagged to the
floor and sat there with his chin on his knees.

'No point,' said the Doctor.

'Don't be daft! You can fight this, Doctor. I know
you can fight it! We have the safe-cracker now,
remember? That means we can –'

'Oh, that,' said the Doctor. 'I don't think that will
work.'

'What do you mean? You said –'

'It was in that chest for about a hundred years. It's
probably seized up by now. And, anyway, I've been
thinking, and I think we shouldn't interfere.'

'Can you even hear yourself?'

The Doctor looked up at Amy. 'Don't you see?' he
said. 'This terminal was placed under quarantine for a
reason: to keep the Desponds contained. If we lift it –'

'We have to lift it! We have to let all these
people go!'

'But we'd be letting the Desponds go too. They'd
be bound to slip aboard a ship and –'

'They won't! We'll make sure they don't.'

'And then they'll spread across the galaxy.' The Doctor shuddered at the thought. 'I almost let that happen. What could I have been thinking?'

'You were trying to help,' said Amy. 'You're the Doctor. It's what you do.'

The Doctor shook his head. 'Not any more. I want a quiet life from now on. No risks. You know, I can't remember the last time I just sat and watched the telly with a nice plate of cheese on toast. Do you think I should buy some comfy slippers?'

'Oh, right,' said Amy. 'That does it!' She took the Doctor's arm again. She hauled him to his feet. 'So what do you want to do?' she challenged him. 'Give up?'

'Yes, I think we should,' said the Doctor.

'Get back into the TARDIS and just . . . just fly out of here?'

'That would probably be for the best.'

'What about Janie, Doctor? What about Mr and Mrs Henry, and the others? You'd be leaving them to starve!'

'I suppose I would.'

'You promised them you'd save them!'

'I know. I know I did. But I've tried my best, and I can't do it.' The Doctor put his hands on Amy's

84

shoulders. He looked right into her eyes, and she saw only despair in his gaze. 'So, I think you're right,' he said. 'We should leave.'

'No! No, Doctor, I didn't mean –'

But the Doctor was already heading for the TARDIS.

'Nothing more we can do here, Pond,' he said over his shoulder. 'It's hopeless!'

Cap's spaceship had probably once been white. Now its hull was all corroded and patched up with black tape. Rory certainly wouldn't have wanted to fly in it – not that flying outside of it was any better.

Rory flapped about helplessly in zero gravity. He wanted to be sick. He dropped his toolkit and it floated away from him. Fortunately, Roger caught it.

The security guard was sticking close to his prisoner.

Roger took Rory's arm. He found a handhold on the side of the ship and used it to pull the two of them along the hull towards the nose.

Rory found that if he faced the ship he felt better.

The ship was attached, via a white docking tube, to the spaceport itself. The spaceport looked like a giant white top. Its 'spindle', Rory guessed, was the Space Traffic Control tower. He wondered if the Doctor and Amy were in there now.

He wondered if they were watching him.

There were portholes in the side of the spaceport. Through these, Rory could see the lights of the departure lounge. He could see people in there, and he thought he could make out Mr and Mrs Henry. He focused on them.

It was when he looked the other way that Rory had problems. It was when he looked out at the endless darkness of space. That was when he felt alone. That was when he felt small. That was when his stomach insisted on performing somersaults.

Roger had reached an engine pod. He thrust the toolkit into Rory's chest. 'Go on then, genius,' his voice came over the helmet radio. 'Show us what you can do.'

Rory almost floated right past the pod. He had to grab hold of it to steady himself. He opened the toolkit and looked at the collection of different-sized spanners and screwdrivers and gadgets he didn't even recognise.

He looked at the engine pod: an egg-shaped bulge on the side of the spaceship, roughly where the wing would have been on an aeroplane. He had planned to tinker with the engines a little, maybe tighten a few nuts and bolts – at least it would have looked like he was trying. He now realised, however, that even this was beyond his talents.

There must be a tool in the kit that will open up the pod, Rory thought – but he had no idea which one it might be.

Roger was glaring at him impatiently. Any second now, he would realise the truth: that Rory really couldn't help him. And then what?

If Rory was ever going to act, it had to be now.

He thrust the toolkit into Roger's face. Its contents spilled out, more gently than Rory had hoped they might. They floated around the security guard's head, doing him no harm but at least keeping him distracted for a second.

Rory pulled himself along his lifeline as fast as he could. He had to get back on board the ship before Roger could recover and radio Cap in the cockpit.

In his haste, however, he overshot the airlock door.

Rory could hear Roger screaming in his ear. 'He's making a break for it, Cap. Cut the lifeline. Cut the lifeline!'

He heard Cap's much calmer response. 'Will do, son. Cap out.'

Rory managed to turn himself round. He pulled on his lifeline again, but the cable went slack in his hands. He kept tugging on it anyway, out of desperation, and reeled in the cable until he was holding its burnt end. He stared at it in horror.

His momentum kept him drifting backwards past the tail of the ship. He tried to get back. He kicked his legs like a swimmer, but he had nothing to push against.

'I warned you that would happen!' Roger's radio voice sneered in Rory's ear.

Rory was drifting even faster than he had thought. With every second that passed he floated further and further away from Cap's spaceship. *And from the spaceport too*, he realised.

He felt as if his heart had frozen in his chest. *They did it*, he thought. *Roger and Cap actually did it . . . They've sent me hurtling off into outer space!*

The Doctor paused in the TARDIS doorway. He turned back to Amy.

'Coming?' he asked.

'You can't be serious,' said Amy.

'Deadly.'

'But what about Rory? Apart from anything else –'

The Doctor shrugged. 'He's probably in some kind of trouble. Nothing we can do.'

'That's my husband you're talking about!'

'And if we go looking for him, we'll probably get into trouble ourselves, and then we'll never get out of here and . . . No. This is how it has to be. No choice.

I'm leaving. Right now. Are you coming with me, Amy Pond?'

'No,' said Amy. She folded her arms stubbornly. 'No, I'm not.'

The Doctor nodded. 'Okay,' he said.

He slammed the TARDIS door in Amy's face.

'And you won't go either,' Amy shouted through the door. 'I know you won't, because whatever those monsters have done to you, whatever they've taken from you, you're still *you*. You're the Doctor. You're my Doctor.'

The TARDIS engines wheezed and groaned into life. The light on its roof flashed. Amy's heart pounded.

'You're my Raggedy Doctor,' she cried, 'and I'm Amelia Pond, the girl who waited, and I know you'd never abandon me. You always come back for me!'

The police box began to dematerialise. Amy went to hammer on the doors. Her fist went through them.

The engine noise was building to a raucous trumpeting.

The TARDIS was leaving without her.

Chapter 10

Adrift

Amy could see right through the TARDIS now. It was almost gone.

Then something wonderful happened. The TARDIS came back.

Its blue box shape became darker and more solid before Amy's eyes. The noise of its engine faded and the blue light on the roof went out.

The police-box doors opened. The Doctor was leaning against the doorway. He looked wretched. 'I don't think I want to go,' he said.

Amy grinned with relief. 'You see?' she said. 'You can't ever leave me. You're stuck with me, buster. You and me forever.'

'Help me,' said the Doctor.

'Always,' Amy promised.

***

Rory fought the urge to panic.

It wasn't easy – he wanted to scream – and he was still drifting further and further out into space. He needed to think fast.

Maybe someone in the spaceport will look out of a porthole, he thought. *Maybe they'll see me out here and raise the alarm – before I drift out of sight!*

He had pleaded for help over his helmet radio, but had got no reply. Either Roger was ignoring him or Rory was already out of his radio range.

He wondered how much oxygen he had left in his tank. *Not much, I'll bet!*

No one was going to help him. Rory had to help himself. He had to find a way to brake – or, better still, to reverse the direction of his flight.

Only one way occurred to him, and it was incredibly dangerous.

Rory felt he had no choice. He turned his back to the spaceport. He was careful to use only tiny movements, so he wouldn't send himself into a spin.

He felt along the tube that connected his oxygen tank to his chest unit. He found the end of the tube and he twisted it.

He pulled the air tube out of its socket and aimed it in front of him like a fire hose. Rory couldn't see the jet of oxygen that rushed out of the end of the tube, but he felt its effects. His stomach heaved as he was propelled backwards like a rocket.

He collided with the spaceport, hard.

If it hadn't been for the padded spacesuit, he might have been badly hurt. As it was, his ribs ached and it took him half a minute to find his breath – and, by that time, he had lost a great deal of oxygen.

Rory clung to the side of the spaceport with one hand, as he tried – and failed – to reconnect his air tube with the other. When the tube stopped fighting him, he knew it was too late. His oxygen tank was empty. Now he had only whatever air was left inside his helmet – he had to get inside the spaceport immediately!

He looked for a way in and, to his relief, he spotted one: an airlock door. All he had to do was reach it . . .

Rory struck out towards the door. He found plenty of handholds and footholds on the spaceport's side, and he climbed from one to the next, careful never to lose contact for fear of drifting off again.

By now, he had certainly been noticed. A mass of curious passengers had been drawn to the departure-lounge portholes to watch Rory's halting progress across the outside of the spaceport.

He was starting to feel light-headed again.

Is it my imagination or is it getting hard to breathe?

He was sure he wasn't going to make it. Then, at last, the locking wheel of the airlock door was in Rory's hands. He spun it round and yanked open the door. He pulled himself into the airlock and slammed the door shut behind him.

Rory's chest ached. He could see dark spots on the edges of his vision. But, as he sagged to his knees, he heard the most beautiful sound in the world: the sound of an air pump activating.

Rory was still weak at the knees as he stumbled into the spaceport departure lounge. He was grateful to be alive, though, and to be breathing warm, sweet air.

He had left his helmet behind in the airlock. He dropped into a red plastic seat and began to strip off the rest of the spacesuit.

'So, this is where you've been hiding yourself.' Mr Henry had appeared in the seat beside Rory.

Mrs Henry sat at his other side. 'Mr Henry and I have been worried about you, dear,' she said. 'You missed out on all the excitement.'

Mr Henry peered closely at Rory. 'Did the Desponds get you? Oh, yes. They fed on you, didn't they?'

'No, actually,' said Rory. 'The Desponds didn't feed on me.'

'Are you sure?' Mr Henry frowned. 'Because you look pretty hopeless to me.'

'I'm not . . . the Desponds haven't fed on me! I've been . . . I was on board one of the spaceships, actually, with that security guard, Roger.'

Mr and Mrs Henry looked at each other. There was fear in their eyes.

'Well, aren't you going to ask me?' said Rory. 'Aren't you going to ask me, "What were you doing on board a spaceship, Rory?"'

The Henrys said nothing.

'No,' said Rory. 'You don't dare ask, do you? You don't want to know, in case the answer gives you hope. Well, you don't have to worry about that. Roger and his friend Cap, they have enough hope for all of us – and, if someone doesn't stop them, they're going to tear this spaceport apart with it.'

The Doctor had gone back into the TARDIS. He had been in such a hurry, though, that he had left his key in the door lock. *I'll take that*, decided Amy, snatching it on her way past. *It'll be safer with me for the moment!*

The Doctor was already at the console. She ran to join him. 'Er, what do you think you're doing?' she asked.

He was flicking switches and pushing buttons. He

turned to Amy with an intense stare. 'Stop me!' he breathed.

He was setting flight coordinates. He was trying to leave again.

'Doctor, no!' cried Amy. She got between him and the controls. She wrestled his left hand away from them, but he reached round her with his right.

'I can't help myself!' said the Doctor. 'Whenever I think about Terminal Four Thousand and the Desponds, it's like –' He was dashing around the console, operating controls as he went. Amy couldn't keep up with him. 'It's like a yawning great chasm in my stomach. No, a void. It's like a void. An aching void. Of despair. And I can't stand it, Amy. I have to get away from it!'

Amy lunged at the Doctor. She grabbed his head in her hands. She planted a big kiss on his lips.

The Doctor reeled away from her, aghast. 'Wh-what did you just *do*?'

'I gave you something else to think about.'

'It's just any excuse with you, isn't it?' the Doctor spluttered.

'Oi, less of the complaining, please. I'll have you know, I'm an excellent kisser.'

'You're also married. And . . . and human. And . . .'

The Doctor sighed. He wandered over to the nearest set of steps and sat down. He buried his face in his hands.

The kiss had worked. It had distracted the Doctor from the controls. Amy almost wished it hadn't. She hated to see him, of all people, like this. His boundless energy had left him. He looked defeated.

'You were right, Amy,' said the Doctor. 'There's no point in our leaving. We'd only wind up somewhere worse. Best we just stay here, in the TARDIS, where it's safe. We should probably stay in here forever.'

It was just as Rory had feared.

Cap and Roger were both in the cockpit of Cap's ship – Rory could hear their muffled voices. He took a deep breath and pushed open the cockpit door.

Cap was sitting in the pilot's seat. Roger stood at his shoulder. He had changed out of his spacesuit and back into his uniform.

They both turned and gaped at him in surprise. Roger went for his gun.

'You're supposed to be dead!' exclaimed Roger.

'And you're supposed to be a security guard,' said Rory. 'It's your job to protect people, not to kidnap them and throw them out into space and –'

'You should have stayed away, son,' Cap drawled.

'You were going to do it, weren't you?' said Rory. 'You were going to start the engines and blast your way out of here!'

'And we still are,' said Roger.

'Course,' said Cap, 'I'd be happier if you'd souped up the engines like you were supposed to. But Roger here had this notion for a new fuel mix that might –'

'I won't let you,' said Rory. 'I won't let you risk everyone's lives.'

'And how do you plan on stopping us?' sneered Roger. He cocked his gun.

'Got any bullets for that thing yet?' asked Rory.

Roger blanched. 'There're still two of us to one of you,' he said.

'Not this time,' said Rory. He could hear footsteps padding up behind him. 'This time, I brought some friends.'

Rory hadn't found it hard to get two Desponds to follow him in here. He had just had to hope they would.

He stepped aside now, and allowed the two creatures to waddle past him into the cockpit. Cap leapt from his seat and Roger shrank against the bulkhead in horror.

Rory was relieved. He had taken a big gamble.

He had gambled that Cap and Roger – so hopeful

about their escape plans – would be a bigger lure to the Desponds than he was. He had been right.

Rory faltered in the doorway, as the Desponds advanced on Cap and Roger.

'I'm sorry,' he said. 'I couldn't think of another way to . . . I had to make you lose hope in your plan, so you wouldn't . . . I mean it. I'm sorry.'

Rory closed the door behind him. He leaned against it, to make sure it stayed shut.

From inside the cockpit, he could hear the Desponds snarling and growling. He could hear the hopeless cries of their prey.

Then, after a minute or so, there was silence.

Chapter 11

Super Sonic

Rory could still hear Roger and Cap's screams in his mind.

What choice did I have? he asked himself. *Someone had to stop them!*

At least the Desponds were leaving him alone now. No doubt they had sensed his low spirits and knew he would be no feast for them.

Rory had asked the Henrys for directions to Space Traffic Control – he had to find Amy and the Doctor. He had just passed the TARDIS where it sat near the luggage carousels when he heard a familiar voice calling his name. He turned and saw Amy standing in the TARDIS doorway. She was beckoning to him.

He could already feel his hopes rising as he ran to join her. 'What's going on?' asked Rory. 'What are you doing in here?'

'It's the Doctor,' said Amy, ushering him inside, then closing the TARDIS door behind them.

'You aren't . . . we aren't leaving already? But what about . . . ?'

Amy looked across the control room. Rory followed her gaze. He saw the Doctor sitting on a step with his head in his hands.

'Oh,' said Rory. 'You mean he's . . . the Desponds?'

Amy nodded. Cautiously they approached the Doctor together.

'Come on, Doctor,' said Rory with forced cheer. 'Can't sit around here all day. You've got work to do. Monsters to fight. Last-second saves to, er, carry out.'

The Doctor didn't respond.

Amy sat down beside him. 'What can we do?' she asked.

'Nothing,' said the Doctor. 'There's nothing you can do. There's no hope.'

'Of course there is,' said Amy. 'There's always hope.'

'Not this time.'

'The last time I saw Janie, she was almost optimistic again,' Amy went on. 'This feeling, this hopelessness – it wears off, Doctor.'

'It doesn't feel like it will. Maybe it'll be different with me.'

'Yeah,' said Amy. 'Maybe it will, cos if anyone can

beat this it's you. You've got . . . normally, you're just bursting with hope. It's like . . . it's like an inexhaustible commodity with you, Doctor. And I know the Desponds could never have taken it all. There must be some hope left in you, somewhere.'

'I'm tired,' said the Doctor. 'Tired of fighting the monsters. What's the use? They always come back. There are always more monsters.'

'He does have a point there,' said Rory.

Amy shot him a look. 'Not helping.'

So Amy and Rory waited. It was all they could think to do. They just waited, and hoped – hoped that the Doctor would recover in time.

The minutes crawled by.

Rory paced around the console anxiously. Amy sat beside the Doctor, holding him tight, until at last he stirred and took out his sonic screwdriver. He began to adjust it.

'Yes, that's it, Doctor,' said Amy. 'That's the spirit!'

The Doctor threw the sonic screwdriver down. He buried his face again. 'It's no good!'

'What? What's no good?' Amy picked up the sonic screwdriver. She pressed it back into the Doctor's hand. 'What were you trying to do? Tell me, Doctor.'

'A stupid long shot,' he muttered. 'It would never have worked.'

'What do you mean? Of course it would've. Your plans always work. Well, almost always. And especially when there's sonicking involved. Sonicking is cool. That's right, isn't it, Doctor? It's almost as cool as . . . as bow ties and fezzes.'

The Doctor looked down at the sonic screwdriver.

'Sonicking is cool,' he conceded. 'Oh, but I tried this before – finding a sound frequency that'll repel the Desponds.'

'Sounds like a good idea to me,' said Amy. 'Sounds like a fantastic idea!'

'Thing is,' said the Doctor, 'I can't do it here. I'd have to try out different sound frequencies on the Desponds themselves. And if I tried the wrong one . . .'

'What'd happen?' asked Rory.

'I could bring the Desponds to me. It's what happened before.'

Amy snatched the sonic screwdriver from the Doctor. 'I'll do it.'

'Whoa,' said Rory. 'Wait a second! Do you even know how to?'

'I was watching what the Doctor did. Twist this bit here to change the frequency, push this button here to make the sound. It's not so hard.'

'Yeah, okay,' said Rory. 'But the Desponds –'

'Someone has to do something,' said Amy. 'That's

104

the problem with this place. No one's doing anything.
No one dares hope in case the Desponds feed on
them – but if no one has any hope, then how can
anyone ever escape from here?'

'I'll come with you,' offered Rory.

'No,' said Amy. 'Stay here with the Doctor. Try to
cheer him up. And keep him away from the controls
until he's feeling more himself. I've had an idea!'

Amy stepped out of the TARDIS. There were no
Desponds in sight.

She pressed the button on the sonic screwdriver
and it emitted a high-pitched shriek that set her teeth
on edge.

Amy stayed close to the TARDIS – she was ready
to run back inside if she had to. However, no
Desponds appeared.

'Okay,' she said to herself. 'Not attracting the
monsters. That's something.'

Amy started walking. She turned the corner into
the empty main concourse where the check-in desks
were and saw a Despond at the far end, beneath a sign
for the spaceport food court. The Despond had
overturned a rubbish bin and was playing with the
spilled contents. Amy could smell the rotting waste
from here.

She approached the dog-like creature on tiptoe. She was halfway across the concourse when it noticed her. It looked up from the bin, its nose twitching.

Amy aimed the sonic screwdriver at the Despond. She activated it again.

The sonic shrieked as it had before, but the Despond appeared unaffected.

'Okay,' said Amy. 'Don't panic. Plenty of time yet.'

She twisted the sonic screwdriver and pressed the button.

This time, the Despond yawned, and Amy caught a glimpse of its feeding tentacle with the little mouth on the end of it. The Despond began to approach her unhurriedly.

Amy backed away. She tried another sound frequency, then another. The Despond kept on coming.

Amy could no longer hear the sonic screwdriver. The sounds it was making were too high-pitched for her ears to detect.

Suddenly the Despond froze. It whimpered. Then it roared.

The Despond came charging at Amy. It was foaming at the mouth.

Amy was so startled that she dropped the sonic screwdriver and it skittered across the tiled floor. She stooped down to retrieve the device, then held it up

to the oncoming Despond, but there was no time
to try another sound frequency. She ran for it
instead.

The Space Traffic Control tower, she thought. *Got to
make it inside!*

She leapt through the door, and turned to shut it in
the Despond's face. *Oh no – too late!* she realised. *The
Despond's too close behind me!*

The Despond barrelled through the door, knocking
Amy over. She landed on the spiral staircase that led
up to the top of the tower. The Despond lunged at her
throat.

Amy kicked it in the stomach.

The Despond fell back. Amy pushed herself to her
feet and scrambled up the stairs. She rounded the first
bend, then she froze in horror.

There was another Despond on the staircase above
her. She was surrounded.

The Desponds closed in on her. Amy shrank
against the wall, fumbling with the sonic screwdriver.
She gave it a good twist and raised it above her head.
Then she closed her eyes and pressed the button.

The Desponds yelped and mewled; they sounded
as if they were in pain. They turned and scampered
away from Amy.

Amy let out the breath she had been holding in.

She kissed the sonic screwdriver. 'Sonicking *is* cool!' she said to herself.

Then she continued up the staircase. She went carefully, because one of the Desponds had disappeared in that direction. She kept that button on the sonic firmly pressed down.

She reached the top of the stairs and found the security door to the Space Traffic Control room half-closed. It was jammed by a chair.

Amy crouched down and peered underneath the door . . . and came eye-to-eye with the missing Despond. It had retreated into the circular control room, just as Amy had expected; there had been nowhere else for it to go.

Amy raised the sonic screwdriver once more, the button still firmly pressed down. The Despond howled and backed as far away from her as it could.

She crawled into the control room, then stood up. The Despond had taken cover underneath an instrument console. Keeping her back to the wall, Amy walked slowly round the room. The Despond trembled as she approached it.

She was careful not to get between the Despond and the exit. She didn't want to think about what the creature might do if it was cornered.

At last, the Despond bolted: it ran under the security door and disappeared down the stairs.

Amy waited until she was sure it was gone, then she laid the sonic screwdriver on the ground and began to search for the tannoy controls.

The passengers were even more subdued than normal. Many of them had returned to their seats, while others were shuffling around aimlessly.

It was always like this after a raid, thought Janie. With the fighting over, they were left to contemplate what they had gained – which, for most of them, was nothing. They were all still trapped here.

Janie was treating a young man with a cut under his eye. She had just used up the last of her antiseptic spray; her flight attendant's first-aid kit was almost empty.

Three melodic chimes rang out from above her head – the public address system. Janie didn't even bother to look up this time. She wouldn't be tricked into hoping again.

'Erm . . . so, okay, yeah. Your attention please.'

Janie was surprised to hear Amy's voice.

'This isn't a passenger announcement,' said Amy. 'I just wanted to say something, and this seemed like the best way to reach all of you. I want to tell you all a story. It's a sort of a fairy tale, really. It's about a . . . a Raggedy Doctor who travels to different worlds in a magic blue box. And I think you're gonna want to hear it.'

Chapter 12

Someone to Believe In

'Erm . . . so, okay, yeah. Your attention please.'

Rory had just turned on the TARDIS's scanner. He had wanted to see – and hear – what was happening outside, in case Amy was in trouble.

'Doctor. Hey.' He shook the Doctor. 'Do you hear that? That's Amy. On the tannoy. She must have reached Space Traffic Control. She's all right.'

The Doctor didn't respond.

Rory listened to Amy's voice. 'She's saying something about . . . a fairy tale, I think. About . . . oh, right. Yeah. Of course. About her Raggedy Doctor. What else?'

'Heard it,' said the Doctor.

***

'Once upon a time,' Amy continued her story, 'I was seven years old, when the Doctor crashed in my back garden. I looked out of my window, and I saw . . .'

As she carried on speaking, she could see the departure lounge on the security monitors. A handful of passengers had stopped to listen to her; most were ignoring her. They could still hear her voice, though – short of covering their ears, they couldn't escape it.

Amy related her first impressions of the Doctor, as he had climbed out of the crashed TARDIS; how he had seemed so wise and so kind and so funny, and how it had been impossible not to trust him. She talked about fish custard and a mysterious crack in her bedroom wall.

Amy had told this story so many times by now that she knew it by heart.

Rory knew the story too. He could almost mouth the words along with Amy.

He wrinkled his nose when she reached the fish custard part. 'Did you really do that?' he asked the Doctor. 'Did you really eat – No, never mind.'

The Doctor looked at Rory dolefully. 'What is she doing?'

'Oh, the usual,' said Rory. 'The same thing she did most days throughout our childhood, and when we

dated, and on our wedding day: she's talking
about you.'

'But why?'

'You tell me,' said Rory. 'She's laying it on a bit
thick, don't you think? I mean, considering we just
got –' He caught the Doctor's eye and shut up, then sat
down beside him. 'Amy did say something, actually.
About how people had to hope. And, if you remember,
Doctor, in the departure lounge, *you* said –'

'I said that people who get to know me –'

'You said that they – *we* – would always have hope.'

'I did say that. I remember saying that. I was so
wrong.'

'No. No, you weren't wrong, Doctor. I might not
always . . . I mean, you might not always be able to
tell, but . . . you give me hope. No matter how bad
things might get sometimes, you've always –'

'She's telling them about me,' the Doctor realised
at last.

'Yes,' said Rory. 'Yes, she is. Amy's telling everyone
about you. She's letting them get to know you, Doctor,
so that they can start hoping again.'

'Let me tell you about hope,' said Amy. 'Because I
know a thing or two about hope. For twelve long
years – over half my life – I hoped to see the

Doctor – my Raggedy Doctor – again. Even when I had everyone telling me . . . They said he wasn't real. They said I must have made him up. They said I should forget about him.

'But I couldn't do that. I couldn't give up on the Doctor. He had said he would come back for me. He had promised. I trusted him. So I waited, and I hoped.

'And then, one day – one amazing, brilliant day – the Doctor was there. He had kept his word. And everything I'd ever hoped for – everything I'd dreamt and much, much more – it all came true for me.

'And do you know what? All the waiting, all the hoping, it was worth it! It was so, so worth it!'

'You don't believe this nonsense, do you, Mrs Henry?'

Mrs Henry started at the sound of her husband's voice. 'Oh. No, dear,' she said. 'No, of course I don't. Nonsense? What nonsense? I wasn't even listening to it.'

But she *had* been listening – and, all across the departure lounge, other people were listening too. They were listening and talking about what they had heard – about the Doctor – and some of them were remembering the tall, floppy-haired man in tweed who had appeared in their midst earlier. The man who had fought the Desponds. Some of them were saying they had seen a blue box, just as Amy had described it. And some of them – a handful to begin with, but others soon followed – were wandering out into the baggage claim hall to see this blue box for themselves.

'It won't work,' said the Doctor.

Rory looked at the scanner screen. He saw the first few passengers arriving outside the TARDIS, staring at it in awe. 'I think it already is,' he said.

'They'll only make themselves targets,' said the Doctor, 'for the Desponds.'

'But there are only twelve Desponds, remember,' said Rory. 'And how many people out there? About a hundred and sixty? And I bet some of them, they can't have been fed on in days. They *can* still hope.'

'If they dare,' said the Doctor.

'If someone gives them a reason to try.'

'I can't be that person. I'm just a . . . I'm just an idiot with a blue box and a bow tie. And nice hair. I do have nice hair.'

'That's the spirit, Doctor,' said Rory. 'And you don't have to give them hope. Amy's doing it already. She has enough hope for all of us.'

It was working. Amy could see it on the security monitors.

A crowd was forming around the TARDIS. The gathering passengers were still confused, uncertain; they didn't know what had brought them here – or, if they did, they were denying it to themselves.

Some people, having made the trek to the TARDIS doors, had already lost their nerve and turned back.

Most of them – both there and in the departure lounge – were waiting. They were waiting to hear more. So Amy had to keep talking. She had to tell them more stories.

Fortunately, she had plenty to tell.

She hadn't rehearsed these new stories as she had the first one – she had been too busy living them. All the same, the words came tumbling out of Amy's mouth. She told her audience about *Starship UK*, and about Winston Churchill and the Daleks.

She told them about the Weeping Angels. 'So, here I am, right,' she said, 'with these statues – these deadly living statues – all around me, and I'm blind. I mean, I'm literally blind. I can't open my eyes or I'll die. Sounds hopeless, right? *Wrong*. Because I felt the Doctor's hands on mine. I heard his voice asking me to trust him.'

Amy talked about vampires in Venice. She talked about the Silurians, the Krafayis and the Cybermen.

She talked about all the times she had faced great danger, and all the times the Doctor had come through for her.

And, the more Amy spoke, the more people seemed to listen.

The crowd around the TARDIS was growing by the second. Its mood had changed, too, becoming more confident, expectant.

There was just one problem.

The Desponds were beginning to take notice, too.

Janie had been waiting for this. She had been dreading it.

Two Desponds were prowling along the edge of the departure lounge. They were approaching the steady stream of people heading for the baggage claim hall.

Janie drew her knees up to her chest, resting her heels on her seat. She closed her eyes. She didn't want to see what happened next. She waited for the screams.

Then she opened her eyes again.

No one had been attacked. In fact, the Desponds had backed off. One of them was scampering away. It hid under a chair.

They were afraid, Janie realised. Something had made the Desponds afraid!

Could it be possible? she wondered. Could Amy have been telling the truth after all? Could there actually be . . . ? *No*, she told herself firmly. *Don't finish that thought!*

All the same, Janie found herself rising to her feet. She found herself joining the stream of passengers. She was just being curious, she told herself. She only wanted to see what was happening out there.

She wasn't expecting anything.

Rory had noticed the Desponds' odd behaviour too.

He could see one of the creatures at the far end of the hall – it was keeping its distance from the crowd around the TARDIS. He pointed this out to the Doctor.

The Doctor – to Rory's surprise – stood up and joined him at the scanner screen.

'Yeah,' he muttered. 'Makes sense, I suppose.'

'What makes sense?' asked Rory. 'Why aren't the Desponds attacking?'

'A surfeit of hope,' said the Doctor.

'What?'

'The Desponds can overeat. We saw it after the riot. They can gorge themselves on hope till they're sick. And, right now, they're sensing more hope in this spaceport than they have in some time. It must be making them nervous.'

'So they're keeping their distance?'

'For now,' said the Doctor. 'They're afraid that once they start feeding they won't be able to stop. It won't last, of course. Overeating is better than starving.'

'But for now,' said Rory, 'it's safe out there. Everyone is safe.'

'As long as they stay hopeful,' said the Doctor.

'So there *is* some use in hoping, after all.'

The Doctor looked at Rory. He was about to say something when a shout went up from outside the TARDIS.

'Doctor! Doctor! Help us, Doctor!'

The voice was a lone one at first, but it was soon joined by many more. The crowd's pleas grew in volume and merged into a rhythmic chant.

'Doctor! Doctor! Doctor!'

The Doctor stuck his fingers in his ears. 'I'm not the one they want.'

'But it's your name they're calling,' said Rory.

'I can't. What if I let them down again?'

'You won't,' said Rory. 'The only way you'll do that is if you keep hiding from them. That's your public out there, Doctor. They're waiting for you to show yourself – and I know you wouldn't want to disappoint them.'

Chapter 13
Fight or Flight

The Doctor emerged from the TARDIS to whoops and cheers.

He was overwhelmed. He stared at the sea of faces before him. Such hopeful faces. He thought they must have the wrong man. He opened his mouth to tell them so.

But then the Doctor remembered something.

He could feel the enthusiasm of the crowd, like a physical force. It washed over him. It re-energised him. They were chanting his name. And the Doctor *remembered*.

He remembered who he was.

Amy was watching on the security-camera monitors.

She watched as a grin tugged at the Doctor's lips.

She watched as he straightened his shoulders and stood tall again. *Result!* she thought.

Her throat was dry from all the talking she had done; she needed a glass of water. As she turned to leave the Space Traffic Control room, she caught her breath.

A Despond had slipped into the room behind her and was sneaking up on her. The creature froze when Amy spotted it. It shifted its weight on to its back claws, about to pounce, and let out a low, menacing growl.

Amy lunged for the sonic screwdriver. She snatched it up from the office chair she had left it on. She pointed the sonic screwdriver at the Despond and activated it.

The Despond kept coming.

Amy took the sonic screwdriver in two hands. She pressed on the button with both thumbs as hard as she could.

Still nothing happened.

No shrieking sound. No bright green light. The sonic screwdriver was dead.

A Despond dared approach the passengers outside the TARDIS. A few people on the edge of the crowd were starting to look worried.

'Oh, don't mind him,' said the Doctor. 'That's as close as he can get. TARDIS force field, you see. I extended it around us. It's invisible – an invisible force field. But it'll keep the Desponds away while we chat.'

The crowd relaxed. The Doctor raised himself on tiptoes to count them.

'So, how many of you are here? About half, I'd say. Half the people in the spaceport. Okay. Could be better; could be worse. Let me answer the question you're all asking yourselves: yes, I can get you out of here. There's just one condition.'

The lone Despond slunk away as the crowd pressed forward, eager to hear more.

'Everyone gets saved,' said the Doctor. 'That's it. That's my condition: no one gets left behind. Not even if they want to be. Not even if they're hiding, curled up in a corner, begging to be left alone because they've no hope left.

'We're all in this together. That means we have to work together and watch out for each other. No more petty rivalries. Those of you hoarding food, share it with the hungry. Those with first-aid skills and equipment, do what you can for the wounded. Those of you who can fly a spaceship, we'll be needing you shortly. Now, then . . .'

The Doctor surveyed the crowd again. He spied a

familiar face. 'Janie Collins!' he exclaimed. 'I'm glad you could make it. Everyone knows Janie, right? Good. Because she'll be in charge of the evacuation.'

Janie shifted uncomfortably on the spot.

'I want the rest of the flight attendants to report to Janie,' said the Doctor. 'I want every passenger in Terminal Four Thousand accounted for and assigned to one of the three spaceships docked out there. I want each of those ships to have a crew.'

'What about the rest of us?' someone asked.

'The rest of you . . . Okay, there is some bad news. Just a bit. A teensy-tiny little bit.' The Doctor took a deep breath. 'I was lying about the TARDIS force field.'

A gasp of horror went up.

'But it's all right,' said the Doctor, 'because you lot, you can protect yourselves. You all saw that Despond just now. You saw how it retreated with its tail between its legs. Well, you did that – all of you – by sticking together. You did it by hoping together.'

'He's right,' someone spoke up. 'The Doctor's right.'

'Remember when the Desponds appeared?' someone else said. 'Remember that security guard – what was his name? Roger? He shot one of them . . .'

'The Desponds are just dumb animals. If we all stood up to them . . .'

'There are more of us than there are of them . . .'

'Problem is, we've been too busy squabbling with each other and . . .'

'They can't drain all of us at once!'

Rory had stepped out of the TARDIS beside the Doctor. He murmured in the Doctor's ear, 'Doctor, have you noticed? Amy –'

'Yeah,' said the Doctor. 'I noticed. She stopped talking.'

'She should have made it back by now,' said Rory. 'I'll go up there and see –'

The Doctor held Rory back. 'No,' he said. 'I need you here.' He nodded towards the crowd. 'They need you here. Things could still get nasty.'

'How do you mean?' asked Rory.

But the Doctor was already in motion, threading his way through the crowd. People tugged at his sleeve. They asked him where he was going. They pleaded with him to stay. The Doctor pulled clear of them. He produced the spider-shaped safe-cracker from his pocket and brandished it for all to see.

'I'm going up to Space Traffic Control,' announced the Doctor. 'I'm going to end the quarantine of this spaceport. In forty minutes or less, or your money back.'

The crowd was stunned into silence. He could hardly blame them.

'Oh, yeah,' said the Doctor. 'One more thing. When I said we would be needing pilots – that would be now, in fact. At least three of them. To prepare for departure.'

The Doctor turned on his heel. He marched away towards the control tower, encouraged along his path by a thunderous wave of applause.

Amy gave the sonic screwdriver a shake. It rattled.

She remembered dropping it downstairs in the main concourse. What if she had broken it? What if she had loosened something inside it?

Without the sonic screwdriver, she was helpless.

The Despond leapt at Amy.

She moved at the same time, pushing an office chair into the creature's path. The Despond collided with the back of the chair and staggered back, winded.

Amy ran for the exit, but the Despond beat her to it. She fell back into the round room. The Despond kept its beady eyes fixed on her, and came at her again. It leapt up on to the chair this time, using the seat as a springboard to Amy's throat.

Taken by surprise, Amy threw up her hands and shrieked. The Despond flew at her. Its feeding tentacle lashed her cheek and left a patch of cold, green slime in its wake.

The Despond clawed at Amy's face. She pushed it away from her, and it fell towards an instrument panel. There was a *bang* and a bright white flash.

The Despond slid off the console and hit the floor, dead. It took Amy a moment to take in what had happened. The creature had been electrocuted!

Her eyes were drawn to the line of text scrolling across a tiny read-out screen.

ALIEN INFESTATION DETECTED AND NEUTRALISED.

Amy looked down at the Despond and felt a lump forming in her throat. In death, it didn't look like a dangerous monster; it looked like a harmless pet.

The passengers returned to the departure lounge, this time with a new sense of purpose – and the lounge soon buzzed with activity.

Janie had gathered all the flight attendants together, as the Doctor had said. They were drawing up lists.

A crew had already been assembled. They were buttoning up their uniforms, straightening their ties. They headed for one of the idle spaceships, but they found a Despond in their path. It lay in front of the airlock door, licking its paws.

Five young men came forward. They had armed themselves with sticks and chairs. They surrounded the Despond. They poked at it and jeered.

The Despond didn't like being treated in this way. It climbed to its feet and snarled at its tormentors. When that didn't work, the creature backed away from them.

The men formed a human wall between the Despond and the flight crew. The grateful crew boarded their ship and shut the airlock door behind them.

A group of around twenty passengers swarmed to the portholes. They waited for over a minute.

Then a rousing cheer broke out as the spaceship's running lights came on.

Mr and Mrs Henry found Rory by the washrooms.

'You look to be at a loose end, dear,' said Mrs Henry.

'I'm . . . supervising,' said Rory defensively. 'What about the pair of you, anyway? I didn't see either of you at the meeting.'

'Oh, we don't get involved in business like that,' said Mr Henry.

'We don't like to get our hopes up,' Mrs Henry agreed.

'Not that we don't wish you all the very best of luck.'

'It has been a long time, hasn't it, Mr Henry?'

'Indeed. It must be two months at least since the last escape attempt.'

'There is one thing though, dear,' said Mrs Henry. 'We did say we would ask.'

Rory looked at the couple suspiciously. 'What is it?'

'We were talking to some well-mannered young chaps over there,' said Mr Henry.

Rory followed the direction of his nod. He saw the five young men who had warded off the Despond; they were looking over at Rory expectantly.

He had a very bad feeling about this.

'It's just, they know you arrived here with the Doctor,' said Mrs Henry.

'And they saw you talking to us earlier,' said Mr Henry, 'and they wondered . . .'

Mrs Henry leaned forward and whispered, 'They've come up with a plan, you see, and they were hoping – I mean, *thinking* – they were thinking you might help them.'

From behind his back, Mr Henry produced a walking stick.

He handed the stick to Rory.

'They were thinking you might join them,' said Mr Henry, 'on a Despond hunt.'

Chapter 14
Hijack

'Blimey!' exclaimed the Doctor. 'What happened here, then?' He looked at the dead Despond on the floor of the round control room. 'Never mind,' he said. 'I get the gist.'

'Did you bring the safe-cracker?' Amy was still shaken, but trying not to show it.

The Doctor held out the spider-shaped device. 'No more wasting time,' he said.

'What can I do?' Amy asked.

The Doctor ducked beneath a console. 'Find Rory,' he said. 'He could use your help. You know what happened the last time he was left on his own.'

'Right,' said Amy. 'It's good to have you back, Doctor.'

'Uh-huh.' The Doctor wasn't listening; he was too busy wiring the safe-cracker into the console's innards.

Amy got down on her hands and knees to crawl under the security door.

'You should keep the sonic screwdriver with you,' said the Doctor. 'For protection.'

'Ah,' said Amy. 'Yeah. I meant to say, actually. About the sonic . . .'

Rory had found a Despond.

It was huddled under one of the red plastic seats in the departure lounge.

He prodded it with Mr Henry's walking stick. It abandoned its makeshift shelter and looked at Rory warily.

It's more nervous than I am, he thought.

For the hundredth time, Rory wondered how he had been roped into this. The plan was simple enough. It even made sense. The objective was to trap as many Desponds as possible behind closed doors – and out of the way – before the spaceships began to board.

This meant that, to begin with, somebody had to lure a Despond into the duty-free shop – and everyone had agreed that Rory, as the Doctor's friend, was the man for the job. Well, of course they had!

The Despond was growing in confidence. It was beginning to realise that Rory was alone, which meant that it could feed on him safely, without risk of overeating.

Rory backed away slowly, and the Despond followed.

He reminded himself that he had done this before: he had led two Desponds on to Cap's ship. He knew exactly what to do. He just had to keep his cool.

The Despond quickened its pace. Rory discouraged it with another prod of the walking stick. He had reached the duty-free shop now.

He backed through the doorway, trampling debris underfoot. He turned his head quickly over his shoulder and saw Mr and Mrs Henry standing behind the tills.

'What are you two doing in here?' he whispered.

'We're just watching, dear,' said Mrs Henry.

'Mrs Henry and I are rather curious to see if this scheme of yours works.'

'We don't care either way, mind.'

'No, indeed not,' Mr Henry agreed. 'We aren't hoping for anything.'

The Despond faltered in the doorway – perhaps it had somehow sensed what was waiting for it inside the shop. Rory *had* to lure it in.

'Here, boy,' he said, pointing to his own throat. 'Nice, um . . . fillet of Rory for you, packed with juicy hope . . . although not too much hope, because we all know that's bad for you. Just a small hope that what I'm doing here might not be as completely insane as it seems, although it probably –'

The Despond lunged at Rory with an ear-splitting howl. It was much faster than he had expected.

He leapt back, stumbling over an upturned shelving unit before falling on to his back. Rory couldn't see the Despond any more, but he could certainly hear it. He swung Mr Henry's walking stick in a blind arc, but missed his target: the Despond ducked under the stick and jumped on top of Rory.

It dug its claws into his chest.

Then its feeding tentacle shot out and attached itself to Rory's throat.

Amy was on her way back to the departure lounge.

She passed the TARDIS and came to the security gate, where she found a man leaning against the wall. He had tightly curled hair and a thin moustache. Amy recognised his face, but couldn't recall his name.

'You're the Doctor's friend, aren't you?' said the man.

'I'm Amy.'

'Got a message for you, from your husband. He said he was waiting for you inside the box.' The man nodded towards the TARDIS.

'Oh,' said Amy. 'Right. Thanks, um . . .'

The man peeled back the lapel of the jacket he was wearing to reveal a security guard's uniform. 'Roger,' he said. 'Roger McDowell. Spaceport Security.'

Rory's fellow Despond hunters sprang their ambush. The five young men leapt out from behind the still-standing shelves, and waved their makeshift weapons at the Despond.

It retracted its feeding tentacle and tried to run, but found itself surrounded.

What's more, someone had smashed a perfume bottle and the scent was confusing the Despond.

Rory climbed to his feet. He felt giddy after his close escape. He raised Mr Henry's walking stick in case he had to defend himself.

The Despond was pivoting on its single front leg, snapping at anyone who dared get too close to it. Two of Rory's allies had a blanket, and they cast it over the Despond, then fell upon the blinded creature and raised their sticks to hit it.

'Enough!' cried Rory. 'That's enough!'

The hunters withdrew reluctantly. The Despond had stopped moving, but it was still conscious – they could all see it trembling through the blanket.

Mr Henry stepped forward. 'What on earth have

you stopped for?' he demanded. 'You have it at your mercy! Kill it! Kill it before it can –'

'No,' said Rory. 'There's no need.'

'No need? After all the suffering these monsters have caused us?'

'Mr Henry is quite right, dear,' said Mrs Henry.

'Give me that blessed stick. I'll do the job myself if nobody else will!' Mr Henry tried to snatch his walking stick back.

Rory held on to it. 'The plan was to trap the Despond,' he said, 'not kill it. Well, we've trapped it. All we have left to do now is get out of the shop and close the doors – both doors – behind us.'

Mr Henry wasn't happy. He grumbled something to himself, but he did back down. His wife put her arm round him and they began to head for the door.

Then the Henrys stopped suddenly in their tracks – there were two more Desponds in front of them.

'Back door!' Rory shouted. 'Quick!'

One of the hunters was ahead of Rory. He ran to the fire exit at the back of the shop, and yanked it open – only to discover a fourth Despond behind it.

The hunter recoiled. He tried to close the door, but it was too late: the Despond was already through it. The hunter abruptly fell back to rejoin Rory and the others.

'Where are they all coming from?' cried Mrs Henry.

'It's like the Doctor said,' Rory realised. 'The Desponds are empathically linked. When we hurt that first one, it must have brought the others running.'

'I knew it,' Mr Henry stormed. 'I knew we should have killed the filthy beast!'

'There's no way out!' cried one of the hunters. 'We're caught in our own trap!'

The Desponds were closing in around them.

Amy knocked on the TARDIS door. There was no answer. She hoped that nothing was wrong in there.

Then she remembered that she still had the Doctor's key. She opened the door, but when she looked inside she could see no sign of Rory in the console room.

Before she had a chance to wonder where he could be, she heard the sound of footsteps running up behind her – fast. She started to turn just as Roger grabbed hold of her, clamping his hand over her mouth so she couldn't cry out. He pushed her into the TARDIS.

Amy struggled and managed to break free. She rounded on Roger. 'What do you think you're doing?'

Roger pulled a gun on her. 'I'm getting out of here.'

'We all are,' said Amy. 'We're all getting out of here.'

'No – I'm getting out of here *now*. In this – what

did you call it? This magic box of yours. And you're going to pilot it for me, or –'

'Hang on,' said Amy. 'Didn't someone say you'd run out of bullets?'

Roger lowered his gun, frustrated. 'Does everyone know about that?'

'All right. Fun's over,' said Amy. 'Let's go back outside, wait for the Doctor to lift the quarantine and we'll say no more about –'

She tried to leave, but Roger got in her way. 'I know what you're planning,' he said. 'You want to get rid of me. You want to feed me to the Desponds like your husband tried to.'

This was news to Amy.

'I had a plan,' Roger went on. 'I had a spaceship and a pilot. Now he's useless. I'm only lucky the Desponds filled up on his hope and didn't feed on me too.'

'We've got spaceships,' said Amy, 'and pilots.'

'And a dozen Desponds running about the place,' said Roger. 'Don't you think we've tried to escape before?'

'It'll be different this time,' said Amy.

'I'm not taking that chance. If this box does half of what you said it does . . .'

Amy shook her head firmly. 'Not a chance, pal,' she said.

'We could just slip away, just the two of us.'

'I couldn't fly the TARDIS even if I wanted to. If you'd listened more closely to my story, you'd know that. The Doctor's the only one who can –'

'I don't believe you!'

'Well, newsflash for you, Roger: I don't care if you believe me or not!'

Amy went for the door again. She pushed Roger aside.

'I . . . I'll do it myself then,' said Roger. 'I'll fly this thing myself. It can't be that hard to work out the controls.'

He ran up the steps to the console.

'Roger, no!' Amy cried after him. 'You don't know what you're doing. You could –'

'Then help me,' Roger said. He flicked a few switches. 'Show me what to do.' He pulled a lever. 'Because until you do I'm just going to keep –'

The TARDIS made a stuttering, coughing sound, and the floor beneath Amy's feet shifted. The glass-like rotor in the centre of the console shuddered violently.

Amy raced up to the TARDIS console. She yanked Roger away from it, hard enough to send him sprawling.

'What did you do?' she yelled at him. '*What did you do?*'

Chapter 15
Cornered

The Doctor had wired the safe-cracker into the computer system, and was now waiting impatiently for it to do its work.

He needed something to keep his hands busy. He picked up the broken sonic screwdriver, which Amy had left behind, and swiftly took the device apart.

He soon found the problem: just a loose wire. Normally, of course, he would have used the sonic screwdriver to fix it! He searched his pockets, and dug out an old stick of chewing gum from the 1970s.

It'll do the job, he decided. He sat down, cross-legged, on the floor.

Had the Doctor been less absorbed in his task, he might have glanced at the security-camera monitors behind him. He might have seen the TARDIS in the baggage claim hall. He might have seen the blue light on its roof beginning to flash.

'Mr Henry!' Mrs Henry wailed. 'Hold me!'

The Henrys, the five young hunters and Rory stood back-to-back in the ruins of the duty-free shop. Four Desponds circled the group, sizing them up. Any second now, they would choose their first victim.

Mr Henry acted first.

He gave the hunter next to him a firm push. Taken by surprise, the young man stumbled forward. He tripped over a Despond and landed on his hands and knees.

The Desponds pounced on him.

'What are you doing?' cried Rory.

'Saving our skins,' Mr Henry retorted. 'Now, while they're distracted!' He grabbed his wife's hand and ran for the fire exit.

The hunters tried to drive the Desponds away from their friend, but they weren't having much luck. A feeding tentacle had already found the unlucky victim's throat.

Another Despond broke away from the pack. It cut in front of the fleeing Henrys, bringing them to a startled halt.

Mr Henry looked at Rory, and Rory saw an evil glint in the old man's eyes.

'Oh no you don't,' he said as Mr Henry tried to push him.

'If you had any decency,' said Mr Henry, 'you'd sacrifice yourself for the rest of us. It's your fault we're in this predicament after all.'

'How is it my fault?'

Rory had only just managed to detach himself from Mr Henry when another Despond came snapping at his ankles. He swiped at it with Mr Henry's walking stick, and the Despond withdrew.

'Anyway,' said Rory, 'I've had a better idea.'

Along the side of the shop, a row of full-length windows looked out on to the departure lounge. Rory turned and flung the walking stick at the nearest window and it smashed right through. He was sure the Henrys would go for the hole he'd just made, luring the Desponds through after them into the full check-in lobby. He just prayed that when the Desponds came across that many hopeful people at once, they wouldn't feed on them.

The TARDIS's engines were screeching and grinding.

Amy stared at the bewildering array of controls on the console. She wished she had paid more attention when the Doctor was using them.

'There has to be a brake on this thing,' she muttered.

Her eyes were drawn to a large lever in the down position. Roger's hand had been near that lever. Had he pulled it?

Amy had to do something. She pushed the lever back up. The TARDIS gave one final judder and fell still.

Roger had picked himself up. He approached the console once more, but Amy pushed him away again. 'Listen to me, you idiot,' she said. 'This is a complex alien machine. You can't just . . . you could have got us both killed! Or stranded anywhere in space or time.'

'I don't care,' said Roger. 'Anywhere is better than Terminal Four Thousand.'

'Yeah? You fancy materialising in the heart of a sun, or . . . or being stranded in prehistoric times? Or –'

Roger lunged for the controls, but Amy stepped into his way yet again.

'Seriously,' she warned him. 'I will hurt you.'

'Is that –' Roger was looking past Amy – 'is that where we are?'

She thought it might be a trick at first. She glared at Roger suspiciously.

Then she turned. She saw that the scanner screen

had been left on . . . and it was no longer showing an image of the baggage claim hall!

Just as Rory thought, the Henrys made for the broken window, and a Despond bounded after them.

The route to the fire-exit door was left clear. Two hunters gave up the struggle with the other three Desponds and ran for it.

The monsters had finished with their first victim – but they weren't satisfied yet. They were taking their chance to eat again while they could.

One of them tackled Mrs Henry and caught the trailing end of her floral-patterned dress between its teeth. Mrs Henry shrieked as the Despond pulled her over. She landed face down and flailed about helplessly.

Mr Henry turned back for his wife. When he saw the Despond clawing at her, however, fear froze him to the spot.

'I'm sorry, my dear,' he said. He turned and dived out through the broken window.

Rory had been turning this way and that, not sure what to do. Now he spotted an intact perfume bottle. He snatched it up and threw it. The bottle smashed on the floor beside Mrs Henry and her Despond attacker dissolved into a sneezing fit and let go of her completely.

Rory ran up to Mrs Henry and hauled her to her feet. She was totally unresponsive: she had closed her eyes tight and was whimpering and moaning. Rory also discovered she was as heavy as she looked; he had to half carry, half drag her through the debris. He bundled her out through the window, then stumbled after her.

Mr Henry was waiting for them in the departure lounge. He had recovered his walking stick and picked up a red plastic chair. Mrs Henry fell into his arms, howling.

Mr Henry brushed her aside. He set his chair down in front of the shop. He climbed up on to it.

Rory realised what he was doing. 'Wait!' he cried. 'There are people still in there.'

With the end of his walking stick, Mr Henry had hooked a steel security shutter and was pulling the shutter down over the broken window.

'The Desponds have them,' Mr Henry insisted. 'We can't help them now.'

'You heard the Doctor,' said Rory. 'No one gets left behind.'

'They shouldn't have provoked the Desponds. They brought this fate upon themselves!'

Mr Henry stepped down from his chair. He started to push the security shutter the rest of the way down, but before he could close it fully Rory ducked underneath it – back into the duty-free shop.

Inside the shop, one Despond was still rolling around sneezing. The other three were worrying at the two remaining hunters.

Rory arrived just as the hunters pulled over a shelving unit. It landed on top of one of the Desponds, pinning it down. The other Desponds appeared to share their fellow's distress and shied away from the men who had caused it.

The hunters seized the chance to rescue their fallen friend. They ran to him and gathered him up, then made for the front door, carrying him between themselves. The Desponds watched them go, but didn't follow.

Instead, they sniffed the air, sensing a better prospect.

The Desponds turned on Rory. They were between him and the front door, and the fire exit was too far away for him to reach before they caught him.

Rory backed up to the window, even as Mr Henry slammed the steel shutter down over it. He tried to lift the shutter from this side, but it had locked into place.

Rory hammered on the shutter, shouting for someone to let him out. No one came. He was trapped – trapped in here with four hungry Desponds, two of which were now advancing upon him, slavering and licking their lips.

Typical, thought Rory. *I rushed in here to save someone else, and now I'm the one who needs saving!*

The safe-cracker pinged. It had found the security code for the spaceport computers.

AWAITING INSTRUCTIONS, said the read-out screen.

The Doctor stood up. He returned the repaired sonic screwdriver to his pocket. 'Hello again, computer,' he said. 'This is your alien infestation speaking. And yes, I do have some instructions for you – since you asked.'

The Doctor flexed his fingers eagerly.

Oh no, thought Janie. Everything had been going so well! Almost all of the passengers, staff and flight crew in the spaceport had been checked in. Only a few people were missing, and a group of volunteers had gone in search of them.

And then a walking stick had come flying through the duty-free shop window, followed a moment later by Mr Henry. A few seconds after this, his wife and

Rory had also clambered out through the hole in the glass.

The passengers didn't know what was happening. Some of them were drawn to the shop to find out; others ran as far away from it as they could. As the passengers ran, the Desponds began to stir again.

Janie could see five of them – no, six. They lurked in the corners of the departure lounge, watching – for now.

Other people saw the Desponds too, and they froze or backed away or just sank to their knees. Their raised hopes had been warding off the Desponds, but that was no longer so: with every passenger who gave in to fear or despair, the creatures grew bolder. They stood a little bit taller; they drew a little bit closer.

Janie dropped her clipboard and sat down with a sigh. It was her own fault, she supposed, for believing in the Doctor. She ought to have known better. She shouldn't have got her hopes up.

Then a man shouted 'Look!' and pointed up at the monitors above their heads. All of the passengers followed the direction of his pointing finger.

The departure boards were updating.

Janie didn't know what it meant at first. She only saw that the list of endlessly delayed flights – a list that hadn't changed in five long months – had disappeared.

In its place, only three flights were listed, and next to each of those flights were two magic words – two words that Janie hadn't seen in what felt like forever: NOW BOARDING.

He's done it, Janie realised. *He has actually done it!*

The Doctor had kept his word. The quarantine of Spaceport Terminal 4000 was over!

Chapter 16
Flights Now Boarding

'What's everyone standing around for?'

Janie recognised the Doctor's voice. She shook herself. She had been staring at the departure boards for at least a minute, hardly able to believe her eyes – and she wasn't the only one.

Then she remembered the Desponds, and looked around for them. Most had gone; she just saw the back end of one as it retreated into the first-class lounge.

The renewed hopes of the passengers had repelled the creatures again.

'I said why is everyone standing around?' The Doctor strode into the centre of the crowd. 'I thought you all had flights to catch!'

That spurred them into action. Within seconds, the departure lounge was a hive of activity once more, and Janie found herself at the heart of it. Everyone wanted to be sure their names were on her list; they wanted to know which ship they were leaving on.

Rory stepped out of the duty-free shop. He wrestled the faulty sliding door shut. He looked around, bewildered.

Everything was as it had been before. Even the Henrys were acting as if nothing had happened. Queues were forming at the airlock doors for the docked ships, and the Henrys had joined one of these.

The Doctor was there. He had just collared a pair of security guards. 'First-class lounge,' he said. 'There's a Despond in there. If you're quick, you can board up the doors and trap it in there.'

'We, ah, also trapped four more,' said Rory. 'In the shop.'

'Yeah, I saw,' said the Doctor, 'on the cameras. Shame you almost caused a panic in the process. Classic Rory!'

'Hey,' said Rory. 'You're the one who got yourself bitten. I'm just saying.'

The Doctor was making his way along the

departure lounge, stopping to peer through each porthole in turn. 'Aren't you going to ask?' he said.

Rory hurried to keep up with him. 'Aren't I going to ask what?'

'How you got out of there. Last thing I saw, you were backed up against a shutter with two Desponds eyeing up your throat.'

'They just sort of backed off,' said Rory. 'You did that, I suppose?'

'I rekindled the passengers' hopes,' said the Doctor. 'And, since there was a crowd of passengers outside the shop . . .'

Rory understood. 'The Desponds could sense them, even through the shutter – like before. There was too much hope for them. Doctor, what are you doing?'

'I'm looking for something.'

'Out there? In space?'

'Out there.' The Doctor came to a halt. He pointed through a porthole. 'In space.'

Rory followed the Doctor's finger. He felt his stomach sinking. He could see a familiar object drifting amongst the stars.

The TARDIS.

Amy rotated the view on the TARDIS's scanner screen. At first, she could see only space. Then, a large white spinning-top shape came into view: the spaceport.

Amy could have cried with relief.

'No! I won't go back there! You can't make me go back there!'

She had forgotten that Roger was behind her. The fight had quite gone out of him, though – he was more despairing than desperate.

'We aren't going anywhere,' said Amy. 'Thanks to you, we're adrift in space, and I don't know how to get us back. So, you just behave!'

Amy turned back to the scanner screen. At least the TARDIS hadn't gone far.

She just hoped that the Doctor could find it out here.

'What do we do?' asked Rory.

'I don't know,' said the Doctor. 'It depends.'

'Depends on what?'

'On who's at the TARDIS controls right now. Have you seen Amy lately?'

'I thought she . . . you mean she might be . . . ?'

'Could have been worse,' said the Doctor. 'At least I remembered the handbrake.'

'The handbrake?' Rory echoed.

'It's a bit worn,' the Doctor confessed. 'Still. Should

keep the TARDIS within about a mile or so of here, and with minimal time slippage.'

He was rifling through his pockets. He unearthed a toothbrush, a ball of string and a clockwork frog, all of which he offloaded on to Rory.

'Of course, if we could find a spacesuit . . .'

'I'm not doing another spacewalk,' said Rory. 'No way!'

'I seem to have lost my door key, anyway.' The Doctor produced a white plastic card triumphantly. 'Galactic Express!' he said. 'Never leave home without it. Tell you what, Rory, I'll deal with the TARDIS. You stop that fight.'

'What fight?'

'The one about to break out behind me.' The Doctor pointed over his shoulder.

Mr and Mrs Henry were arguing with a pair of flight attendants. Janie had rushed on to the scene and was doing her best to calm things down, but Mr Henry was getting angrier. He was pointing with his walking stick.

A few more passengers began to crowd around, joining in the debate.

Rory groaned. 'Now what?'

The Doctor didn't answer. He had spied a row of payphones by the wall.

He ran over to them and snatched up one of the phones. Then he swiped his card through the reader and began to dial.

'I'm sorry,' said Roger.

Amy turned to him, surprised. He was slumped on a step. 'You what?'

'I said I'm sorry, okay?' he snapped. 'I suppose I got a little . . . frantic.'

Amy grimaced. 'You think?'

'You don't know what it's been like for me,' said Roger. 'You've been here all of five minutes – for me, it's been five months!'

'You're not the only one,' said Amy.

'I know. But I was . . . I was scared, okay? I saw what those monsters – the Desponds – did to people, and –'

'They never fed on you?'

'I never let them,' said Roger. 'The nearest they got . . . it was back at the beginning. I still had my gun. Two of them came at me. I panicked.'

'That was when you shot a Despond?'

'Right between the eyes,' said Roger. 'I also shot two plates in the food court, took out a light fitting and grazed a passenger on the arm.'

He buried his face in his hands. 'Five months I've

spent keeping out of their way. I've been jumping at shadows, sleeping with one eye open. I – I've done things I'm not proud of. And where has it got me? I've no hope left, anyway.'

'It'll work this time,' Amy promised. 'The Doctor will fix this.'

Roger shrugged. 'He can't fix things for me. If I get on one of those spaceships with the others, I'll just be swapping one prison for another.'

'What do you mean?'

'I mean they'll lock me up for sure. It's my fault, you see. It's all my fault. I let the Desponds loose in the spaceport.' Roger looked up at Amy, as though he was expecting some reaction.

But Amy had hardly even heard him. Something else had caught her attention.

'Do you hear that?' she asked. 'Do you hear that sound?'

The TARDIS telephone was ringing.

The tension in the departure lounge had escalated. The Henrys had started it, of course. According to a stressed Janie, they had reacted badly when told they would be in the second group to board their ship and then they refused to leave the queue in which they stood.

This had sparked an avalanche of appeals from the other passengers.

'– been here longer than any of –'

'– those of us who trapped the Desponds should surely get to –'

'– paid good money for a first-class ticket, which I think entitles me to –'

Janie stood firm against these unreasonable demands. She insisted that everyone would just have to wait their turn.

So the passengers turned to Rory, as the Doctor's friend, to overrule her.

They were tugging at his sleeve, shouting in his ear. He couldn't possibly answer all of their pleas at once.

One man pressed money into Rory's hand, trying to bribe him. Another was begging for his sick grandmother to be moved up the passenger lists.

An elegant-looking woman was complaining in shrill tones about the ship to which she had been assigned . . . in fact, Rory realised she was talking about Cap's beaten-up old charter ship, so he could hardly blame her.

He didn't know what to say to any of them.

The passengers began to give up on Rory. They

turned on each other instead, yelling and jabbing fingers.

The Doctor had been right. This was about to turn into another fight.

Rory jumped up on to a chair. 'Please,' he said. 'If everyone could just . . . this isn't getting us . . .' No one was listening to him. 'QUIET!' he yelled.

A hush fell over the crowd. They all stared up at Rory, surprised by the authority in his voice. He had surprised himself too.

'The Doctor put Janie in charge of this evacuation,' he carried on, at a normal volume. 'So if you lot can't listen to her and do as she says, then no one will be going anywhere.'

Too much, he thought. He sounded a bit petulant. In fact, he sounded like his old Year 7 school teacher.

Rory's outburst did have an effect, though: the passengers were doing as he said – even Mr and Mrs Henry were returning to their seats, though not without a few final grumbles. Janie and the other flight attendants took over, and soon they had three orderly queues stretching across the departure lounge.

All quarrels were forgotten, then. A thrill of anticipation hung in the air as the flight attendants opened the airlock doors and the passengers began to file on to the waiting spaceships. *It's working*, thought Rory. *This is actually working!*

He glanced over at the Doctor, who was still on the phone and talking animatedly.

Suddenly Rory heard a scream.

Mr Henry leapt to his feet. 'I knew it!' he bellowed. 'I knew this would happen!'

The Desponds were back.

They were coming from all directions, and there were six of them. They were barking and snapping and foaming at the mouth. Rory had never seen them so worked up before.

The Desponds fell upon the passengers.

All hell broke loose.

Chapter 17
A Desperate Battle

Amy dashed around the console room with the phone tucked under her chin. She was following instructions from the Doctor.

'Now,' said the Doctor, 'disengage the temporal dislocation combobulator.'

'The what?'

'Looks like the front panel of a clock radio. Second button from the left.'

'Yeah, I see it. Gonna have to put the phone down.'

Amy left the phone hanging from its cradle in the console by its cord.

She found the control that the Doctor had described. 'Well, that actually *is* a bit of an old clock radio,' she muttered. She hit the snooze button, then picked up the phone again. 'What now?'

'Now,' said the Doctor, 'I have to go. Despond trouble!'

'But –'

'I am going to need you to do one more thing for me: stay on the line, Amy. When I give you the word, you need to pull the big lever. The one to your left now. But not before I give the word! That's important, Amy. The timing has to be spot on.'

'What's happening over there?' asked Amy. 'Doctor?'

But the Doctor had gone.

Amy looked across the console at Roger. He was still sitting on the steps and returned her gaze with a helpless shrug.

Amy pressed the TARDIS phone to her ear. Was it her imagination or could she hear people screaming?

The departure lounge was in chaos.

Everyone was shouting and running. They were either fighting each other and the flight attendants to reach the airlocks, or just panicking and heading for cover.

Rory found himself lost in the confusion. He had already seen three people fed upon. It didn't make any sense! The passengers had been enjoying their highest

hopes yet. Shouldn't that have kept the Desponds
at bay?

He fought his way through the scrum and found
himself next to Mr and Mrs Henry. Mr Henry
grabbed Rory by the front of his shirt.

'Do you see what you've done?' he roared. 'You
and your friends?'

'We had all we needed,' Mrs Henry wailed. 'Our
own two rows of chairs, with our coats and towels to
sleep under, and the washrooms across the way.'

'We said the Desponds wouldn't let us go. We told
you so.'

'Mr Henry is right. You should have listened
to him.'

'They'll feed on all of us now,' said Mr Henry.
'The Desponds will drain us all dry!'

Rory didn't know what to say – and anyway, before
he *could* say anything, someone ran into him from
behind. He was sent flying. He grabbed hold of Mrs
Henry to steady himself, but she shrieked and shoved
him away from her.

A Despond had appeared behind Rory. It was
snarling and spitting.

Rory backed away slowly – and collided with a
group of people who were backing away from a
Despond of their own.

The advancing creatures went for the nearest targets. They snapped at legs with their normal mouths; as far as Rory could see, they weren't using their feeding tentacles.

The Henrys were right, he realised. The Desponds were more intelligent than Rory had supposed. They had eaten enough – but they saw that people were leaving the spaceport, and they were desperate to stop them.

They didn't want to lose their food source.

Rory picked up a chair. He prodded a Despond with it until it let its victim go and rounded on Rory instead. It leapt at him – now its feeding tentacle *was* extended. Rory threw the chair at it, and chair and Despond collided in mid-air. Both dropped to the floor. The Despond got tangled up in the chair legs.

The flight attendants were struggling to close the airlock doors before the Desponds could squeeze through them. If the monsters managed to get on to a spaceship and feed on the flight crew . . . It didn't even bear thinking about.

Rory stumbled over a body and put his hand down to steady himself. The fallen woman was one of the many passengers who had by now been fed upon. She was curled up into a ball, sobbing.

As Rory's hand touched the floor, a Despond leapt at him. It clamped its jaws round his arm. He tried to shake it off, but its grip was too strong.

The creature's teeth sank into his flesh. Extending two fingers, Rory thrust them towards the Despond's eyes, but the creature flinched before his fingers could reach it. It let go of Rory's arm and ran off.

Rory felt a hand on his shoulder. He turned. The Doctor had found him.

'Doctor,' he gasped. 'The Desponds. They –'

'Yeah. I can see that for myself,' said the Doctor. 'I thought this might happen.'

'You did? Great. Thanks for, y'know, the warning.'

'I have a plan,' said the Doctor. 'But you might not like it.'

'I like it,' said Rory. 'I like any plan right now. Anything.'

The Doctor held up the sonic screwdriver. He pushed a button on its side.

'Especially,' said Rory, 'any plan that involves sonicking. You're making that sound, right? The one that no one can hear, but it repels the Desponds?'

'Um, not quite,' said the Doctor.

'Er, what does "not quite" mean?'

'Never did find that frequency,' said the Doctor.

'Amy did, but she never got around to showing me. So, this is the other one.'

'The other what? Oh, no! You don't mean –'

'The other frequency,' the Doctor confirmed. 'The one I found by accident when we first got here. The one that, um, attracts them.'

Rory could hear the Desponds howling. The howls were getting closer.

Now he could see them. They were pushing their way through the crowd, completely ignoring the passengers in their need to find the source of the noise that only they could hear.

Every Despond in the spaceport was closing in on the Doctor and Rory.

'I found them in a cargo-ship hold,' said Roger.

Amy was clutching the TARDIS phone to her ear. She didn't really want to talk – but it seemed that Roger had to get this off his chest.

'It was a routine security check,' he explained. 'The mother must have sneaked aboard at the last port of call. She died giving birth to her litter.'

'The Desponds?' guessed Amy.

'Thirteen of them. Thirteen little puppies. According to regulations, I should have had them destroyed.'

'No.'

'I couldn't bring myself to – there's a storeroom down by the power plant, where no one ever goes. I hid them in there. I looked after them. They ate real food back then. The first time a Despond went for my throat, I thought it was just being playful.'

'What happened?' asked Amy.

'They grew up,' said Roger. 'They developed those feeding tentacles. I . . . I didn't know what to do. Then one of the other guards – a friend of mine – I think she must have heard them whining. She opened the storeroom door.'

'And the Desponds got out into the spaceport,' said Amy.

'Which triggered the automatic quarantine,' concluded Roger.

He stood up and approached Amy. She was ready in case he tried anything again.

'Does the Doctor really have a plan?' asked Roger. 'Can he really end this?'

'I . . . I don't know,' said Amy. 'I was waiting for his word, but –' she looked down at the phone – 'I can't hear a thing. I think we might have been cut off.'

'How many Desponds do you count?' asked the Doctor.

'Five,' said Rory nervously. 'No, six.'

'Plus four in the duty-free shop, one in the first-class lounge, one dead in Space Traffic Control . . . That'll be the lot, then.'

The Doctor and Rory backed away from the advancing Desponds. They were nearing the end of the departure lounge.

'Remember what I said about liking this plan?' said Rory. 'I've gone off it.'

'It's working though,' said the Doctor. He waggled the sonic screwdriver and the Desponds' eyes followed it, as if they were hypnotised.

Behind them, Janie had reopened the airlock doors and was hurrying the passengers through them.

'A couple of minutes more,' said the Doctor, 'and everyone will be safely out of here. Well, everyone but us. Here – catch!' He suddenly tossed the sonic screwdriver Rory's way, and Rory almost dropped it.

'Keep the button pressed down,' said the Doctor. He darted over to the side of the duty-free shop to grab something: a red fire extinguisher.

The Doctor shook the extinguisher. It was empty. He dropped it and grabbed another. At the same time, two Desponds charged at Rory.

The Doctor jumped into their path and blasted them with extinguisher foam. They spluttered and fell back – but Rory could see two more sneaking up around him from opposite sides. The Doctor blasted one of them; Rory vaulted a row of red plastic chairs to escape the other, which was just squeezing under a chair to reach him when it yelped. A jet of freezing-cold extinguisher foam had struck it on the rear end.

Rory scrambled over the chairs to rejoin the Doctor. Together, they backed up to the wall as the Desponds advanced upon them again. The Doctor gave the extinguisher to Rory and took the sonic screwdriver back.

Rory sprayed the foam in a wide arc in front of him. 'There'd better be another part to this plan,' he said. It was then that he noticed the row of payphones behind them.

The Doctor had left one of the phones off the hook. He snatched it up now and shouted into the handset. 'Now, Amy! The lever! Amy? Amy, are you there?'

The Doctor fumbled through his pockets. He found his white plastic card and swiped it through the reader. Then he swiped it again. And yet again. His face fell.

'What? What is it?' asked Rory.

'Out of credit,' said the Doctor.

'And that's bad, right?'

'That's bad.' The Doctor let go of the phone.

'Because if I can't get a message to Amy . . .' He didn't have to finish his sentence.

The six Desponds were straining ever further forward, as if sensing the weakness of their cornered prey. The fire extinguisher sputtered in Rory's hands – it was about to run dry.

'You were right,' said the Doctor. 'This was a bad plan. A very, very bad plan.'

Chapter 18

Departures

'So this is it,' said Rory.

'Looks like it,' the Doctor agreed.

'This is where I'm going to live out the rest of my days. In Terminal Four Thousand.'

'Yup.'

'I'll never think about leaving, even though I can see the TARDIS right outside the window. Even though I know my wife is in there –'

'That's about the size of it.'

'Because the Desponds will have sucked every last drop of hope out of me.'

'There is a bright side,' said the Doctor. 'Two bright sides, in fact.'

He looked across the departure lounge. Rory followed his gaze. The spaceships had finished boarding. Cap's charter ship had disengaged its locking clamps and was already pulling away.

The evacuation was complete. The stranded passengers had escaped.

'And the other bright side?' asked Rory.

He was aiming the fire extinguisher more selectively now so as to preserve its contents. Even so, the white foam was coming out in fits and starts.

'There's no food,' said the Doctor. 'So, the rest of our days won't be all that long.'

The extinguisher was completely empty.

Rory threw it at the Desponds. The gesture bought them about half a second.

Then the six Desponds charged forward.

Amy had hung up the TARDIS phone. She glared at it as if sheer willpower could make it ring again.

'The Doctor gave you instructions?' asked Roger.

'Yeah, he told me *what* to do,' said Amy. 'Just not *when*. He said the timing was important.' Her hand went to the big lever by the phone. She hesitated.

'You should do it,' said Roger.

'But what if I time it wrong? What if I should have waited longer?'

'What if you wait too long?' Roger pointed to the scanner screen. 'Look!'

Amy looked up. 'The ships,' she breathed. 'They're leaving!'

'The Doctor did it,' said Roger.

'He did,' agreed Amy. 'Maybe that's why he never came back to the phone. Maybe the Doctor and Rory are on one of those ships and they don't need this after all.'

She looked at the lever doubtfully.

'Or not,' she said. 'I don't know. What . . . what do you think?'

'I think you've got to have hope,' said Roger.

Amy looked at him, surprised. He was right of course; she just hadn't expected him to be the one to say it.

She nodded.

Roger held up his hand. He had crossed his fingers for her.

Amy closed her eyes. She drew in a deep breath. Then she pulled the lever.

The first Despond leapt at Rory's throat. He managed to bat it away, but the second was right behind it.

The Doctor was under attack too. The other creatures had closed in on their prey, and were keeping the Doctor and Rory contained. There was nowhere to run.

173

Then Rory heard a familiar sound. A wheezing, groaning sound.

A blue haze appeared in the air between him and the six Desponds.

The sound grew louder and the blue haze thicker. A springing Despond was flung back in mid-air by some invisible force.

Then Rory could see the dog-like creatures no longer. The spaceport was gone too. He was standing inside the TARDIS, by the console. The Doctor was still beside him, but now so was Amy, and so was – Rory did a double-take at this – Roger.

The Doctor turned to Amy. 'I thought I told you to wait for my cue,' he said. Then a grin broke out on his face. 'Good job you didn't, though.'

'Good to see you too,' said Amy.

The Doctor ran round the console, operating it with his usual manic energy.

'I don't get it,' said Rory. 'What happened?'

'What happened,' the Doctor explained, 'is that Amy here – clever, wonderful Amy – just flew the TARDIS. Not only that, but her timing was perfect.'

'I think . . .' said Amy. 'Did I just land the TARDIS *around* the two of you?'

Rory noticed the scanner screen. It was showing an

image of the spaceport departure lounge. It was empty now but for the six Desponds.

They were howling and whimpering. A couple lay on their sides, whining pitifully to themselves. Rory almost felt sorry for the creatures. They had lost all hope.

'That reminds me.' The Doctor gestured across the console. 'Amy. The temporal dislocation combobulator. You need to turn it back on.'

'Got it,' said Amy.

'While you're there, you could give the helmic regulator a quick boost and crank up the thermo buffer. Rory? You could . . . well, you could put the kettle on. Or something. Oh, and, Roger – was that your name?'

Roger straightened up, surprised. He started towards the Doctor.

The Doctor held up a hand to stop him. 'Don't you even talk to me!'

Roger stopped in his tracks, then sat back down.

The sound of the TARDIS's engines filled the console room. The image on the scanner screen disintegrated into static. The TARDIS was taking off.

'What are you doing?' asked Rory.

'Concentrating,' said the Doctor. 'This next part is

a bit tricky. I'm going to land the TARDIS inside a moving vehicle.'

The Doctor stepped out of the TARDIS. He was greeted once again by cheers and applause. 'You know,' he said to Amy and Rory, 'I could get quite used to this.'

They had landed aboard a spaceship. It was filled with passengers from the spaceport terminal. They were sitting in rows, all buckled in, and were nibbling on stale pretzels that the flight attendants must have found and distributed.

Rory recognised two of them. 'Mr and Mrs Henry,' he said. 'I'm glad you made it.'

The Henrys shushed him crossly, waving him aside. He was blocking their view of the in-flight movie. Rory scowled at the couple as he moved.

A flight attendant appeared from the cockpit. 'Doctor!' she cried joyfully.

'Janie Collins!' the Doctor exclaimed as Janie flung her arms around him. 'Looking a bit more cheerful now.'

'Thanks to you,' said Janie.

'How about the rest of them? Did everyone make it out?'

Janie noticed Roger hovering in the TARDIS's doorway.

'They have now,' she said. 'Ours was the last ship to leave. We've radioed the other two, and everything is okay with them. A few problems with the charter ship – well, with its owner more than anything – but nothing we need to worry about.'

'Where will you go?' asked Amy.

'Terminal Three Thousand Nine Hundred and Ninety-nine, then everyone can take onward flights from there,' said Janie. 'Estimated flight time is about thirty and a half hours.'

'Thirty and a half hours?' The Doctor's jaw dropped open in horror.

Amy elbowed him in the ribs. 'Behave,' she hissed. 'Remember we can't all go whizzing about the universe in a super-duper police box.'

'I need you to do one more thing for me,' said the Doctor to Janie.

'Anything,' she said.

'Take care of the Desponds – as in look after them. Yeah, I know that sounds mad after all they did to you. I know how they hurt you, but –'

'But it wasn't their fault,' said Janie. 'They just acted according to their nature.'

The Doctor grinned. 'I knew you'd understand.'

'And they're like us now, aren't they? I mean, they're like we used to be. They're stranded in

Terminal Four Thousand, just like we were. And they have no food.'

'Here,' said the Doctor. He showed Janie his psychic paper; anyone who looked at that paper saw what the Doctor wanted them to see.

'Details of an animal-welfare organisation,' he said. 'An *alien* animal-welfare organisation. They'll know what to do with the Desponds.'

'I'll contact them as soon as I can,' Janie promised.

Roger had slipped away. He found himself a seat towards the back of the passenger cabin. He looked surprised when Amy came and sat down beside him.

'I know what you're thinking,' she said.

'I don't know what to do,' said Roger. 'There's bound to be an inquiry. Do I tell them the truth about the Desponds or –'

'You can't take all the blame,' said Amy. 'You tried to do a good thing. I mean, yeah, you broke a few silly rules, but –'

'This'll cost the spaceport company billions in payouts,' Roger cut in. 'Mr and Mrs Henry have asked for the forms already. They'll be looking for someone to blame.'

'You couldn't have known all this would happen,' said Amy. 'Anyway, that company of yours have a lot to answer for too, leaving you all stranded like that.'

'Your husband's looking over here,' Roger commented.

He was right. Rory was giving him the evil eye.

'Don't mind him,' said Amy. 'He doesn't like it when I talk to other men.'

'Um, yeah,' said Roger. 'And I did . . . when I lost my mind for a bit, back there, I did kind of . . . I knocked him out. And then I threw him out of an airlock.'

'You did what?'

'Will you tell him I'm sorry?'

'Yeah, you know what?' said Amy. 'I think you should tell the truth to that inquiry after all. Tell them the whole story. I'm sure they'll be every bit as forgiving as I am.'

They didn't stay long. The Doctor hated goodbyes. So, as soon as he knew he wasn't needed any more, he ushered Amy and Rory back into the TARDIS.

'Random coordinates,' he decided. 'And let's hope we end up somewhere more interesting than a spaceport. Okay, more interesting than *most* spaceports.'

'They will be all right, won't they?' said Amy.

'Who?' The Doctor looked up from the console as if he had forgotten already.

'The passengers. Janie. What the Desponds did to them . . .'

'Worn off already, in most cases. They might have a few bad dreams, but otherwise no lasting effects. Well, look at me: I'm as fit as a flea.'

The Doctor jumped up and down on the spot to prove his point.

'That's a fiddle,' said Rory. 'It's fit as a fiddle.'

'Are you sure?' said the Doctor. 'I always thought it was a flea. Anyway, don't worry about the former residents of Spaceport Terminal Four Thousand. It's like you said before, Amy – hope's an inexhaustible commodity. No matter how bad things might sometimes seem, there's always hope.'

The End

Titles in the series:

The Galactic Fair has arrived on the mining asteroid of Stanalan and anticipation is building around the construction of the fair's most popular attraction – the Death Ride! But there is something sinister going on behind all the fun of the fair: people are mysteriously dying in the Off-Limits tunnels. Join the Doctor, Amy and Rory as they investigate . . .

The Doctor finds himself trapped in the virtual world of Parallife. As the Doctor tries to save the inhabitants from being destroyed by a deadly virus, Amy and Rory must fight to keep his body in the real world, safe from the mysterious entity known as Legacy . . .

The Doctor, Amy and Rory are surprised to discover lumps of moon rock scattered around a farm. But things get even stranger when they find out where the moon rock is coming from – a Rock Man is turning everything he touches to stone! Can the Doctor, Amy and Rory find out what the creature wants before it's too late?

The Eleventh Doctor and his friends,
Amy and Rory, join a group of explorers on a
Victorian tramp steamer in the Florida Everglades.
The mysterious explorers are searching for
the Fountain of Youth, but neither they —
nor the treasure they seek — are
quite what they seem . . .

Terrible tiny creatures swarm down from
the sky, intent on destroying everything on planet
Xirrinda. As the colonists try to fight the alien
infestation, the Eleventh Doctor searches for
the ancient secret weapon of the native
Ulla people. Is it enough to save the day?

A distress signal calls the TARDIS to the *Black
Horizon*, a spaceship under attack from the
Empire of Eternal Victory. But the robotic
scavengers are the least of the Eleventh
Doctor's worries. Something terrifying is
waiting to trap him in space . . .

The Eleventh Doctor treats Rory to a trip to the Wild West, where the TARDIS crew find a town full of sleeping people and a gang of menacing outlaws intent on robbing the local bank. But it soon becomes clear that Amy, Rory and the Doctor are not the only visitors to Mason City, Nevada . . .

An ancient artefact awakes, trapping one of the Eleventh Doctor's companions on an archaeological dig in Egypt. The only way for the Doctor to save his friend is to travel thousands of years back in time to defeat the mysterious Water Thief . . .

People are mysteriously disappearing on Moonbase Laika. They eventually return, but with strange bite marks on their bodies and no idea where they have been. Can the Eleventh Doctor get to the bottom of what's going on?

The Eleventh Doctor and his friends head to the 1966 World Cup final. While the Doctor and Amy discover that the Time Lord isn't the only alien visiting Wembley Stadium, Rory finds himself playing a crucial role in this historic England versus West Germany football match . . .

The TARDIS crew are quarantined in Terminal 4000, where the hideous Desponds have destroyed the hopes of all waiting passengers. Can the Eleventh Doctor and his friends save the day by helping everyone to escape, without succumbing to despair themselves?

The Eleventh Doctor and his companions are on board the *Cosmic Rover*, a spaceship orbiting the water-planet Hydron. Joining the crew, they journey underwater on a scientific exploration. But nothing is as it seems on the high-tech submarine. When a virus infects the crew, the Doctor discovers the ship is hiding a dangerous secret . . .